Starliner

Starliner

Gordon Donnell

iUniverse, Inc.
New York Lincoln Shanghai

Starliner

iUniverse, Inc.

For information address:
iUniverse, Inc.
2021 Pine Lake Road, Suite 100
Lincoln, NE 68512
www.iuniverse.com

ISBN: 0-595-30133-9

Printed in the United States of America

CHAPTER 1

I sat up and took notice when she idled past. A drop-dead blonde doing a slow cruise in a Bentley wasn't something I expected to see on a forgettable night in East L.A. She turned at the intersection and disappeared. I went back to listening to the oldies station and drumming the slow beat of *The Stroll* on the steering wheel.

Three hours had already dragged by. So far, a sixteen year old runaway from Pacific Palisades hadn't shown up with an eighth grade neighbor girl to buy a dime bag of marijuana from a Latino kid who didn't seem to know he was supposed to be hanging out on the empty corner I was watching.

According to the neighbor girl's parents, the boy had done that before, when the Latino kid had been there. The boy's parents had insisted on spending some money to make sure he wasn't still doing it.

The blonde idled past again. I read her license number into my recorder.

She eased her Bentley to the curb and shut it down. The street lamp at the intersection silhouetted her through the glass of cars parked between us. We seemed to be interested in the same corner. She climbed out.

Except for a lack of unit insignia, her jacket was Air Force flying issue; pale green nylon with Day-Glo orange lining. She slung a bag over her shoulder and came straight toward me, like she had spotted me watching her and wanted to make something of it.

I muted the radio and rolled down my window.

"Hello," I said, and caught a whiff of Shalimar as she bent to peer in at me.

"Are you a police officer?" Her husky words rode a rip tide of tension.

"My name is Henry Spain. What's yours?"

"May I see your badge, please?"

"I'm not a police officer, Ms. uh—?"

Her eyes turned to blue ice. There was no reason for her to think I was a cop. Maybe she just needed one.

"Is something wrong?" I asked.

"There's a man in a cream colored station wagon."

She glanced at a parking strip on the far side of the intersection, just beyond the glow of the street lamp. Shadows blended the shapes of individual cars into an angular mass and reduced colors to shades of light and dark. Distance and dimness concealed any occupants.

"What's he doing?" I asked.

"Nothing. He's just sitting there."

"You mean like you and me?"

"He doesn't look right. Somebody should check on him."

She was miffed. I wasn't taking her seriously. She looked stubborn enough to hang around until I did.

"All right," I said. "I'll make you a deal. If you'll tell me your name, I'll go talk to your man."

Impatient fingers rippled against her shoulder bag. She was in no mood to be hit on by a middle-aged cluck in a Volvo that was as old as she was. I waited for whatever was eating her to wear down her resistance.

"Stephanie," she said.

"Stephanie what?"

"St. John."

She stepped back so I could climb out into the cold January drizzle. Judging from the look she gave me, the in-crowd wasn't wearing corduroy trousers this season, or plaid flannel shirts with the cuffs turned back over long-sleeve fatigue underwear. I put on my bomber jacket to try for a little style. It didn't seem to help. Maybe the cargo pockets weren't supposed to have actual cargo in them.

"All right, Stephanie. You point out your man and I'll go talk to him."

"It's Stevie. Everyone calls me Stevie."

I was doing better. I was on the team now. We set off down the street.

It was Friday, and I could hear the bass beat of low riders in the distance, defying the ban. The hours of stiffness in my legs reminded me I was no longer young. I had long since lost any illusion of being tough.

Stevie stopped me and pointed toward the parking strip. One of the cars was a compact station wagon, backed perpendicular to the cinder block wall of a single story building. I could just make out a figure behind the wheel.

"There," she said.

The triumph in her voice said more. She had been right. I never should have doubted her. She sounded ready to charge across the intersection and confront the driver.

I didn't try to explain why that was a no-no. She was twenty something; ready to grab life by the throat and shake it until it gave her what she wanted. I didn't think she would understand how a corporate downsizing or a dissolving marriage could leave someone sitting in a dark parking lot trying to work up the nerve to put a .357 into his mouth and blow his brains all over the headliner of the family wagon.

A minivan started up in the lot of the restaurant where I had been thinking about going for a late enchilada. We needed to get out of the street.

"You can wait in your car if you'd like," I told her.

It wasn't chivalry. I wanted a witness at a safe distance who could call for help if I stepped into trouble. She killed the idea with a determined shake of her head.

"I want to see."

An unlit sidewalk across the street from the building offered the best chance to circle unseen and approach the station wagon from behind. I went that way as soon as the minivan was gone and before anyone's night vision could recover from exposure to the headlights.

Stevie was hot on my heels.

I wasn't sure what I was trying to prove. Maybe I just didn't want to face the fact that my best years and my brilliant future were behind me.

The building fronted on that street and we had to pass under a floodlight when we crossed, but by then we were out of the angle of the station wagon's mirrors and behind the driver's peripheral vision.

A sign said the building was a film processing franchise. The parked cars probably belonged to a night shift working away inside in their hairnets and latex gloves. Which raised the possibility Stevie and I were sneaking up on some weary soul taking a nap during his break. I stopped, suddenly feeling foolish.

"Stevie, that isn't the man you're here to meet."

She stood in the glow of the floodlight, staring at me through an insistent silence. I was turning out to be a big disappointment.

"That car is tan. You saw cream colored because that's what you were told to look for. You saw the driver as a man because you expected to meet a man."

"You said you'd check on him."

Her tone left no doubt that my manhood was under a microscope. I could tolerate being a superannuated knight in rusty armor, but I didn't appreciate being treated like I'd come down with a sudden case of juvenile insecurity.

"First you wanted a cop," I snapped back. "When you couldn't find one, you recruited a total stranger. What has you spooked?"

"Do you want to borrow my pepper spray?"

"No. Thank you."

At close range the butt of a small flashlight would be more effective. I worked mine out of my pocket just in case and slipped between the building wall and the parked cars.

Stevie stayed close behind me.

The station wagon was an older Toyota. Plastic toys were scattered in the cargo area. The rear seat had an empty infant restraint. The man in the driver's seat looked like he might have put his head back against the rest and dozed off. I rapped gently on the glass, hoping to wake him without startling him.

"Excuse me, Sir?"

He didn't wake. I rapped harder.

"Pardon, Senor?"

Nothing. I tried the door.

It opened with a squeak of sprung hinges. The driver rolled against the shoulder restraint. His head drooped. One arm flopped out and hung limp, his fingers an inch above the asphalt. I shined my flashlight on the pallid features of a Latino in his twenties.

His jaw hung slack. His eyes were open and glazed. Indrawn breath told me Stevie recognized the mess coagulated in the hair behind his ear.

"Is he—?"

I got a grip on my nerves, reached in and tried to find a pulse at the man's neck artery. One touch of cold skin and I knew it was futile.

"Yeah." It wasn't so much a word as the air leaking out of me.

Stevie swallowed to keep her stomach down. Survival instinct warned me to start her talking while she was off guard.

"Have you got a cell phone in your bag?"

She fumbled it out and tried to hand it to me. I shook my head. If I'd wanted to make the call myself, I would have dug my own phone out of my pocket.

"Get through to 911," I instructed. "They'll tell you what to say."

I was guessing they would want her home address and telephone number. I wanted them too. I had some questions to ask her when the police finished with us.

It wasn't my night. She had no trouble getting the operator to accept the address and phone number from the building sign. I handed her a business card when she clicked off.

"Stevie, we need to stay in touch until this is resolved."

She shoved the card into her bag with her cell phone.

"How can I reach you?" I asked.

She wasn't listening. She tried to push past me. I caught her by both arms.

"Stevie, do you know that man?"

"I don't want to look at him."

"Who did you come here to meet?"

"Let me go."

Desperation put power into her legs. I had to give ground to maintain both my hold and my balance.

"Come on, Stevie. Tell me what you've sucked me into here. I need to know."

She gave me a swift kick in the shin. I shuffled to avoid a heel shot into my instep. She knew how to fight. I tried to maneuver her into a restraining hold.

A squadrol pulled into the lot and caught us slow dancing. We both froze in the headlights and the surreal flash of blue strobes.

Two uniforms piled out and separated us.

After that events moved with the leaden certainty of official procedure. Police and medical vehicles arrived. Yellow tape was strung. The routine of photographing, measuring and documenting began.

I wasn't looking forward to the trip to Rampart Division. The LAPD had a fat file on me. None of it was flattering.

CHAPTER 2

Stevie was escorted politely into the station. I wound up in a doublewide trailer with the rest of the Friday night overflow. At the next desk a pre-law student was explaining quality-of-life enforcement to the uniform who was filling out his arrest paperwork. The kid thought it meant spanking punks in South Central who had no family values. Or finger-printing the next generation of lowlifes and loading them into the computer for a quick catch when they turned pro. He didn't think a couple of fraternity brothers ought to wind up in the felony prone for trying to crash a high school dance. The cop didn't get it. He probably thought USC stood for University of Spoiled Children.

They were still at it when the investigator arrived. He wore a freshly pressed sport coat over an open collar dress shirt; fashionable blue micro-check with a discreet brown stripe, light starch, delivered on a hanger. Notice to the world that he had his associate degree in police science. His after-shave reeked of ambition.

"Mr. Spain?"

"Yes."

"I'm Officer Enright."

"Pleased to meet you," I said.

I didn't mean it and he didn't hear it. He sat down and opened a monogrammed zipper case on the desk.

"Mr. Spain, this is not your first police contact."

I kept my mouth shut. Some of that contact was uncomfortably current.

"You have been principal in more than one fatal shooting," he persisted.

I could practically hear his twenty credit hours in psychology telling him I should be a basket case from post-traumatic disorder. He consulted his paperwork, probably to find out why I was still running around loose, let alone carrying an investigator's license. I belonged in a halfway house, under close supervision, with a few hours of liberty each day to earn my keep pushing a broom.

"Your psychological profile indicates that under stress you become withdrawn and hostile."

It was Catch-22. I could remain quiet and prove I was withdrawn or argue and prove I was hostile.

"At one in the morning, I'm mostly just tired."

"You must have some emotional reaction. Finding a dead body is disturbing under any circumstances. Even veteran patrol officers are affected."

"I guess it hasn't sunk in yet." I knew it would.

Enright uncapped a razor point pen and printed my name in neat block capitals at the top of a yellow legal tablet.

"All right, Mr. Spain. Let's start with what you were doing in that neighborhood tonight."

I told him about the sixteen year old runaway.

"Who are your clients?" he asked.

"Jerry and Cassandra Freegate."

"The car dealer?"

Freegate's dealerships sold foreign luxury models. His rugged good looks, cutting edge business attire and sincere pledge of dedication to total customer satisfaction were a fixture on local television.

Cassandra didn't appear in the commercials. She had been a dancer in Vegas. Even well into her thirties and dressed down in a long skirt and a loose linen jacket she was a bit much for family audiences.

"Yes," I told Enright. "The car dealer."

"The boy's name?"

"Robbie. Martin Robert Freegate."

Jerry had said he was Cassandra's by a previous marriage. She seemed to think it had been a relationship. The biological father was ten years dead, so I hadn't pressed for any history.

"And you thought staking out a quiet corner in East L.A. was the best way to find him?" Enright asked.

"That was Mr. Freegate's idea."

"What was your idea?"

I chanted the skip tracers' mantra. "Work forward from the last known location. Interview family and friends. Identify habits and interests. Monitor credit card and cell phone bills. Post a reward on the Internet."

"But in this case you took money for an obviously unproductive surveillance."

"Only at Mr. Freegate's insistence." Against my better financial judgment, I had tried to talk him out of it.

"How did you meet Stephanie St. John?"

I told him what had happened. He took careful notes in his neat block printing. It was a simple clerical chore, but he made a production of it, almost a warning. If I deviated one millimeter from the truth, he would have me by the short curlies.

"Ms. St. John is a commercial pilot, is that correct?"

That would explain the flying jacket, but not the Bentley. The car was too rich for anyone who worked for a living.

"She didn't volunteer any information about herself."

"What did she tell you about the Starliner?"

I didn't know whether that was a straight question or some kind of interview control Enright was throwing at me to see if I would spin him a few lies.

"She asked me to check on a man in a station wagon. That's all."

"The responding officers reported the two of you were involved in an altercation when they arrived. What was that about?"

"Finding the body upset her. She tried to leave. I restrained her until the police came."

I was pretty sure there was more to it than that, but until I had a chance to ask Stevie what it was, I felt safer playing ignorant. It didn't require any acting talent.

"Did you know the victim, Mr. Spain?"

"No."

"His name was Eladio Aguilar. He was a first year medical student, with a wife and two children. He worked nights at the photo processing lab where you found him."

Humanizing the victim was a standard part of any police interview. It was meant to soften up the witness before the tough questions began. I let the subject drift.

"Did you hear the shot?" Enright asked.

"I didn't know he'd been shot."

"You saw the wound."

"Only the blood in his hair."

"Did you notice any activity near his car?"

I couldn't recall any.

Enright fixed his eyes on mine and didn't say a word. It was a stress interview technique. Some people aren't comfortable with silence. They start blabbing whatever is on their mind after ten seconds of it. When stony staring didn't get him anywhere, Enright pointed his pen at me.

"You had a ringside seat at Eladio Aguilar's murder."

"I was half a block away, shut inside my car with the radio playing. If the shot had been loud enough for me to hear, people in the photo lab would have heard it too."

"Your car had windows."

"So did the restaurant across the street."

Every word I'd said was true, but I still managed to make it sound like a string of alibis from a man who wondered whether he could have prevented what happened.

Enright wrote slowly, giving me plenty of time to blurt out any guilty tidbits that might be troubling me. "As a professional investigator, Mr. Spain, what do you think really happened?"

It wasn't a serious question, just another page from the police interrogation manual. Treat the subject as a peer. Build his ego. Start him talking. He may say more than he intended.

Stevie had gone to meet a man she knew only by the color and model of his car. She had mistaken the dead man's station wagon for her appointment. That didn't mean the killer had made the same mistake.

"I don't do criminal work," was all I told Enright.

He capped his pen and closed his zipper case. "I think we'll need a polygraph, Mr. Spain."

"Why?"

"You can see how this looks. A man with your record of police contact in the area of a homicide for more than three hours with no witnesses to account for your activity."

"Do you think I shot somebody I never heard of with a gun I wasn't carrying then hung around for three hours waiting for someone I didn't know would show up to come along and talk me into finding the body?"

I didn't like being accused of murder. Enright's glare told me that was no excuse for mocking his authority.

"Do you expect me to believe you were just in the wrong place at the wrong time?" he demanded.

"Yes." It was the story of my life. Someday it was liable to be my epitaph.

"Wait here, Mr. Spain. I'll have your statement typed for signature."

The pre-law student's father arrived while Enright was gone. Everything from his grooming to his cultivated speech suggested money and importance. He tried to explain to the cop that his son never should have been arrested over a harmless prank. Instead he had to listen while the cop went over the charges, the list of agencies available for behavioral counseling and the misdemeanor hearing procedure. Then he had to sign the same forms a welfare mother from Compton would have to sign to collect her wannabe gang banger. The system cut everybody down to size.

I felt small and vulnerable.

Time passed and things slowed down. There was no heat in the trailer, and not many people left. I went from cooling my heels to freezing my tail. As I grew older, the world seemed to be growing cold around me.

My fingers were a nice shade of blue by the time I had a statement to sign. Enright gave me a copy and put the original in his case. The next item was a consent form for a polygraph examination with my name typed under the signature block.

"You are not a suspect, Mr. Spain," he was careful to tell me. "I'm merely advising you that at this time there are outstanding issues regarding your statement."

That didn't mean he didn't think I wouldn't make a good fall-back position if his investigation bogged down and he had to close the case to protect his career. It was just that his legal notification requirements would escalate dramatically if he made the idea official.

"I don't think a polygraph is necessary," I said.

I'd been down that road when I was younger. Passing didn't clear you. It just made the investigators think they weren't asking the right questions.

Enright marked in his neat block printing that I had declined examination. His initials made it official. Another thread in the ever-tightening web of evidence.

"We'll be in touch, Mr. Spain."

The parking lot held cars, but no Bentley. Stevie was long gone. My shin throbbed where she had kicked me. The desk officer just smiled when I limped in and asked for her phone number.

I retrieved my Volvo and drove to my office to find out how good a skip tracer I really was. I needed to locate Stevie. I had to persuade her to tell me what sort of trouble I had blundered into, before I learned the hard way.

CHAPTER 3

I booted up my desk computer and fed it the greater L.A. telephone CD-ROM. Neither S. St. John turned out to be Stevie, and neither was happy with me for rousting her out of bed at oh-dark-thirty on Saturday morning. Most air carriers were staffed around the clock. My fiction about needing an emergency locate on one of their pilots had credibility at that hour, but none of them had Stevie on their payroll. By the time I had exhausted the list, dawn was a red glow behind the skyline. After twenty four hours without sleep, neither my eyes nor my brain were focusing reliably. I settled for posting Stevie's license number to a website.

The site belonged to a crackpot who was bent on ridding the state of internal combustion engines. To finance his crusade, he had hacked into the Department of Motor Vehicles computer. For a modest fee, he would provide a registered owner and address for any California plate.

One thing he didn't offer was a good way to tell Jerry Freegate the police would be calling him about a homicide. Some encouraging news about his missing stepson might make things easier, but it was too early to expect anything. I clicked open my box on the skip trace network just so I could tell him I'd checked.

I wasn't sure what to make of the happy face and the Canadian phone number. The woman who answered told me she was Kathryn Mahoney, Kat for short. She sounded young and full of energy, and a bit short on the common sense and experience it takes to make a living hunting runaways. She had been checking motels for a missing Inuit girl as a favor to a friend in social welfare, and shopping descriptions of the three highest bounties on the network to see if she could make a little money at the same time. The other two were general distribution, just like mine. The chances of any of them showing up where she was looking were the cube root of an orphan's inheritance. So the first place she walked into she found Robbie Freegate trying to feed an American dollar to a Canadian soda machine.

Robbie told her a cyber age version of the usual sad story. His parents didn't understand him. His teachers were on his case. The kids at school weren't cool. He and two friends had seen an ad on the Internet. A Cree Indian medicine man was offering cuttings of the most powerful marijuana ever grown. They headed north, dreaming of parties, babes, cash and more parties, not knowing their medicine man was already in jail.

The joker was actually a Rumanian refugee who gave the suckers a blow of high-grade sinsemilla and sold them garden weed. He thought he was legal because he didn't transfer real marijuana plants. The RCMP booked him for everything from fraud to air pollution and he wound up in the local newspaper's police blotter.

Kat showed the article to Robbie, who by then had split with his two friends and discovered he couldn't surf in Saskatchewan. Home looked pretty good. He just didn't want to make the call.

No problem, kid. Nice Mr. Spain is delighted to make those calls. He gets paid for it.

It was Cassandra who answered. She sounded like she hadn't slept either.

"Good morning, Mrs. Freegate. This is Henry Spain. May I speak with your husband, please?"

"Did you find Robbie?"

"Your son is safe, Mrs. Freegate."

I gave her Kat's name and phone number and reminded her of the amount she and her husband had agreed for a valid locate. Jerry was out for his morning run, so I told her about finding the dead man. She didn't sound bothered by it, but she had probably hit emotional overload. Recovering a lost child tended to push the rest of the world into the background. She had never heard of Stephanie St. John.

I had used up my quota of luck, probably for the rest of the month. I shut down the computer, locked the office and went home bone tired to see what I could salvage of the weekend.

Jerry Freegate held down the first spot on Monday's voice mail. Robbie was home safe. Jerry was grateful. Was I driving the kind of vehicle that would position me effectively with an upper income clientele? Call him. He had a wide range of lease programs. Unfortunately, I had a narrow transportation budget.

The other message was from a Peter Lomax. He had an assignment for me. He also had the kind of diction and grammar that suggested he could afford me. I pressed out his number while I clicked through the weekend spam to check for a response on Stevie's license plate.

"Peter Lomax."

He answered telephones in one of those executive voices that strove for just the right mix of authority and approachability. I could practically smell his breath mints.

"Henry Spain, Mr. Lomax. Returning your call."

"Ahh, yes. Mr. Spain. Thank you. I have a confidential matter I would like to discuss. Can you stop by my office this morning?"

I wanted to be sure it was also a paying matter before I invested any time or travel. I was about to ask Peter Lomax for some preliminary details when I found the mail I wanted. The Bentley Stevie had been driving Friday night was registered to a Harold Lomax of Pasadena.

"Mr. Spain?"

"Where is your office, Mr. Lomax?"

His directions took me to a business park in El Segundo. The building was a sprawling affair of concrete and smoked glass with flagpoles out front and manicured shrubbery to hide the loading docks in back.

I had to wait in the reception area. People came and went, using security badges to open the inner doors. I may have been the only person in the building wearing a coat and tie. I felt conspicuously out of step with modern life. Henry Spain, professional dinosaur.

Things improved slightly when Lomax came to collect me. He also was wearing a coat. No tie, but his shirt had cost money and the cleaners had starched it for him. He looked natural in starch. He was a couple of inches taller than my six feet and he stood straight enough to make it obvious. Forty years had softened whatever athletic fantasies he may once have harbored. I couldn't help resenting his perfect hair.

"What do you folks do here?" I asked after he ushered me through a door and started us along a hallway.

"Prescott is software distribution and fulfillment."

"What does that involve?"

I didn't really care, but talk was habit forming. If I could get him warmed up on trivial stuff, he'd probably keep right on blabbing when we got to his confidential matter.

He didn't need encouragement. He rattled off an impressive list of software companies whose bits and bytes Prescott put on store shelves. They had a room-sized machine that duplicated CD-ROMs and dumped them onto a production line that packed and shrink-wrapped them; all under Draconian security designed to foil that most dastardly of all villains—the software pirate.

"These criminals have no respect for intellectual property." His stern expression suggested neither I nor society at large were doing nearly enough to stamp out this monstrous plague.

The polished round table that dominated his office tried to suggest that he preferred a collegial management style, but his high-backed executive swivel said more. His backdrop was an ergonomic wall unit. The work surface held a high-end laptop computer docked under a big monitor; notice his visitors that he was important enough to travel. I sat down, unzipped my portfolio and got the micro cassette recorder running.

"I'll take no more of your time than necessary," I assured him, and poised a pencil.

Lomax sat back and shifted his executive communication skills into high gear. "My wife, and this is in the strictest confidence, is considering a run for the Los Angeles City Council."

It might have been a bombshell at the right cocktail party. To me it was just general information. Lomax was visibly irked when I didn't bother to write it down.

"Paige is an attorney. She is prominent in civic and legal circles. You may have heard of her."

"I'm sorry. No."

"Not important," he said, dismissing my ignorance with an indulgent wave of his fingers. "What does matter is that political campaigns of late have taken on a very negative tone. Every facet of a candidate's life is minutely scrutinized. The most trivial incidents can be blown up into hysterical sound bites. I'm sure you're familiar with some of the more egregious examples."

Lomax had a large vocabulary, and he liked to exercise it. If he were going to get to the point before my tape ran out and my stomach started growling for lunch, he would need help.

"Your telephone message mentioned an assignment."

"My late mother," he announced, "before her marriage to my father, enjoyed a career as a film actress."

He waited for my reaction.

I didn't have one.

He covered his irritation with a practiced smile. "That period of my mother's life may come under hostile scrutiny if my wife does decide to seek office."

"Possibly," I said, to see if making agreeable noises would move the conversation forward.

"There is no scandal," he said emphatically, "but there is always the possibility that a jealous rival may try to settle an old grudge with some scurrilous lie."

"What would you like me to do, Mr. Lomax?"

"Our purpose in retaining you would be to investigate my mother's background. To prepare us for anything that might emerge from a later, less benign inquiry. To preempt my wife's political opponents, as it were."

I did my best to keep a straight face. Lomax was married to an attorney. She had access to the top background specialists in the city. If this were a legitimate job, he wouldn't waste time talking to a generic skip tracer. Not that I objected. It gave me a chance to start firing questions at him.

"May I have your mother's maiden name, Mr. Lomax?"

"Cynthia Louise Halston," he said, and cut the odds of any relation to Stevie on that side of the family. He removed his rimless spectacles, teasing them off carefully so he wouldn't disturb his hair. "Have you any experience with the concept of partnering?"

"No, Mr. Lomax. I don't. May I have your father's first name?"

A tolerant smile came and went. "As I believe I told you, my mother's career pre-dated their marriage."

"So did their courtship. It would help if I could sort out your father from other men she might have been seeing."

"Harold. My father's name was Harold."

I was so busy suppressing a triumphant grin that I had written and underlined the name before the verb tense registered. "Excuse me. Was?"

"My father passed away two weeks ago." The honest note of sadness in his voice was jarring in the context of his affected speech.

"I am sorry. Was it sudden?"

"A traffic accident. It was widely reported. My father was prominent." Everyone in the Lomax family seemed to be prominent. Except Peter.

"Did your mother precede your father in death?"

"Her final illness was some five years ago."

"Did your father re-marry?"

"No."

"Did he establish an intimate relationship with anyone?"

Lomax teased the spectacles back over his ears and peered at me through the lightly tinted lenses. "Why do you ask?"

I wasn't about to tell him that I was checking my reconstruction of the scenario behind his call. The police would have run Stevie's license plate and contacted the family of the late Harold Lomax to be sure she had permission to use his Bentley. They also would have asked about me, to see if Stevie and I were connected in any way the Lomax family knew about. That might have started the family wondering if we were connected in any way they should know about. As in were we trying to shake down daddy Harold.

"Recent intimates are an excellent source of information about past partners," I said. "Women are always curious about former wives."

"My father was in his eighties."

That made Stevie sound more like an ornament than an intimate. I felt more relief than I should have.

Lomax resumed his management lecture. "The concept of partnering involves collaboration between parties to a contract. You and I will be in close touch during the conduct of your investigation. You keeping me informed of the steps you are taking, and I using my knowledge of my mother's career to guide you."

"Mr. Lomax, my investigations are conducted to strict industry standards. My insurer and bonding agent insist. It's a matter of minimizing legal exposure."

He stared at me. His wife had probably made a few discreet inquiries. I still had some residual reputation as an industrial thug who would do anything for money. The suggestion that I had standards left him speechless. I decided to restore his faith in human frailty.

"Your check for $5,000 will get me started."

"I will pay a fair rate at the satisfactory completion of your work according to the terms I have outlined."

"May I speak frankly, Mr. Lomax?"

"I encourage it. Open communication is the key to successful partnering."

"Why don't you contact one or more of my competitors to either locate an acceptable provider, or satisfy yourself that my terms are reasonable?"

They weren't, of course. I'd thrown out a ridiculously high figure to see how desperate he really was.

"I'm afraid I haven't time for that."

He swiveled his chair to the wall unit and found a leather-bound checkbook in a drawer. He sat with his back to me and talked while he wrote. He wanted to be kept apprised of what I was doing at all times. He wanted my assurance that I would be working only for him. It sounded like he wanted to put me on a leash.

"Is there anything else I should know?" I asked, rather than commit to exclusive service.

He tore out the check and swiveled to hand it to me. "My mother began her film career in the 1940's, when European actresses, particularly Sonja Henie and Signe Hasso, were in vogue. She worked under the name Sigrid Helstrom."

He was turning me loose on an open budget to conduct an unrestricted investigation into potentially sensitive areas of his family background without so much as asking for references. I tucked the check away, closed my portfolio and tried not to look surprised.

"I'll bring my standard contract by for your signature," I said to give him one more chance to object.

"That will be fine."

Lomax escorted me back to reception. On the way he told me about his weekend. He and Paige had gone to an invitation-only reception at the Getty Museum Saturday evening. Sunday he had gone yacht racing. Just as a crew member, mind you. He had sold his own ketch at the end of last season. He was having a custom hull shipped in from Holland. Even when it arrived, it would have to be rigged and fitted with a special keel. No chance to campaign it this season. But he had high hopes for next year.

I was aching to ask him about Stevie. He had given me way too much money just to keep daddy Harold's indiscretions covered up. Some real skeletons were rattling around in the Lomax family closet, and Stevie was involved somehow.

Experience told me to do some checking before I opened my mouth. For once, I listened.

Chapter 4

My first stop was a wobbly plastic chair in front of a public library microfiche reader. A newspaper obituary told me Harold Lomax had graduated from Stanford Law School in 1944, at the height of World War II, and promptly joined the FBI. Apparently he wasn't just looking for a socially acceptable alternative to storming fortified coastlines. He made a career of the Bureau, eventually specializing in foreign police liaison. His last posting was Vietnam. The fall of Saigon in 1975 seemed to have dampened his enthusiasm for government service. He retired and entered private law practice the same year. He was survived by his only child, Peter, and a couple of grandchildren.

There was no mention of how he had come by the money for a Bentley or a Pasadena address, but I did find an article on the accident that had killed him after he left a black tie charity dinner. The driver claimed Lomax had run out in front of his car, giving him no time to stop. His story might have gone down better if his blood alcohol level had tested below the legal limit. The paper didn't report Lomax's blood alcohol, but even stewed to the gills, eighty year old men weren't noted for doing mid-block wind sprints across six lanes of fast moving traffic. Which raised the question of how he came to be hit. I didn't have an answer, so I went back to my office and called a number at UCLA to start the background on Mrs. Harold Lomax.

"Professor Exum, please. My name is Henry Spain."

Roy Lee Exum was an associate in the cinema department. "You've got a nerve," she came on in a chilly Cape Cod drawl.

Our last encounter hadn't been on the best of terms, so I got right to business, before she had a chance to hang up on me. "Sigrid Helstrom, true name Cynthia

Louise Halston. For seventy five dollars an hour and an outside chance of never hearing from me again, what can you tell me about her film career?"

"In connection with what, please, Mr. Spain?"

"Henry. It's a background investigation commissioned by a family member."

"Hold, please."

My kind of music had a solid rhythm line with a blues beat behind it. Several minutes of wispy Viennese waltzes sedated me thoroughly.

She came back, her voice dripping skepticism. "How sure are you about the Louise?"

"It comes from her closest living relative."

A keyboard clicked briefly in the background. "Profound thanks from the academic community. You have just added to the lore of a great educational institution."

"What does your institution have on her?"

"We may have something someday, if anyone ever gets around to assigning a graduate student to research her. For now, you'll have to settle for a filmography."

"Can you give me a sample?"

"1946, played a truck stop waitress briefly brutalized by escaping felons in the epic *Folsom Prison Breakout,* starring nobody you ever heard of. 1947, a nun violated by communist soldiers in the propaganda classic *March of Evil.* No known surviving prints. If she was smart, she burned them herself. Later in '47, blonde goddess of the tropics in the twelve part serial *Biff Kellogg of the Fighting Navy.* Shall I continue?"

It didn't sound like a promising pedigree for the future wife of a Stanford Law School graduate. "Anything available today?"

"Here's the one you want. 1948, *Ambush Road.* Mob girl seeks revenge for the rape of her sister by staging a series of violent robberies against the gangsters responsible. Helstrom played the sister. Her performance drew some favorable notices, but I don't see anything subsequent to indicate she was able to follow up."

"Can I rent this puppy?"

"Buy it for your collection, Mr. Spain. It's your kind of flick. Film Noir. Everyone but Helstrom eats a bullet."

"Is there anyone alive today who might have known her during her film career?"

She ran a cross-reference on cast lists and came up with the name Ramona Benitez and a telephone number. I had time to stop by Peter Lomax's office to get his signature on a contract and deposit his check for immediate credit to my account before I was due at the nursing home where Ramona agreed to see me.

The place was an island of seedy elegance in a neighborhood best visited during daylight hours. I went in under the awning that shaded the main door and was shown through an entry into a lobby where Ramona waited at one of several coffee tables arranged for semi-private conversations.

Perched on a faded sofa, she was a withered pixie wrapped in a flowered robe.

"So very nice to meet you, Mr. Spain."

The hand she held up felt as frail as tissue. I didn't dare squeeze or shake it.

"This is my grand-daughter, Marisol," she said.

Marisol was in her early twenties; thin and dark and dutiful. A business suit, a photo ID badge and a small jaw tight with stress suggested she had stopped by after a long day of trying to cope with impossible corporate expectations. She set a heavy photo album on the table and hovered protectively at the old woman's shoulder.

"Are you a journalist, Mr. Spain," she asked with an edge of suspicion that suggested I had better be at least that.

"Mr. Spain is a private eye."

Girlish mischief danced in Ramona's dark eyes, as if her mind had begun to detach itself from the wasted body in which it was trapped, slipping one by one the tethers of reality.

Marisol gave me a dubious look. "Are you sure you should talk to him?"

"What can he do to me? Take away my freedom and leave me with a panoramic view of the Hollywood Freeway?"

"Dad thinks it's best, Gram," Marisol said contritely. "We all have to work, and you know you can't manage by yourself at home any more."

Ramona patted the cushion beside her and I sat down. "There you have my life, Mr. Spain. I used to get letters from men all over the country describing in the most lurid detail the perverted acts they were going to perform if they ever got me alone. Now all I can do is sit here and wish I had saved the return addresses."

"Gram!" Marisol scolded.

"Be a love and open the book."

The album was old, and the memories there had been visited often. Marisol turned the worn pages carefully to a black and white publicity still. A young Ramona stood on a windblown hill. Her peasant blouse clung to a pair of firm breasts. A loose skirt fluttered up to show as much leg as the censors would allow. Marisol stroked the photo, as if it were one of her favorites.

"Remember *Last Days Of Juarez*, Gram? It was your first picture."

"Not exactly a starring role," Ramona told me, "and probably before your time."

"I do remember you in a film called *Customs House*," I lied. It was a title Roy Lee Exum had given me.

"I was strangled in it, was what I was. With my own scarf. Not that I'm complaining. There wasn't a broad on the lot who wouldn't gladly have been strangled, or anything else, by Horst Bochner." She patted my knee confidentially. "Horst was veddy, veddy continental you know. Continental men are much better with fragrances. At least they were in those days. Horst smelled delicious."

"You were cast in that film with an actress named Sigrid Helstrom."

Years peeled away and Ramona's dark eyes shone. "Sig and I were roommates, Mr. Spain. Even before our movie days. Back during the Second World War, when we were posing for cheesecake and hitting the night spots trying to connect with anyone who could get us into a studio."

"I'll bet you could tell some stories." I gave her a sly wink.

"About Sig?" she asked. "Is she the reason you came to see poor old Ramona?" Her eyes filled with disappointment.

Nice going, Spain. What were the basics of interviewing again? Be patient. Build rapport. Don't rush the subject. It was a little late to enroll in remedial training, so I gave her a big smile and pushed on.

"I'm particularly interested in what you have to say about her. Being an actress yourself, as well as her friend, you have a perspective no one else could provide."

Marisol had a good ear for a snow job. She was about to bite my head off when Ramona patted her hand to stop her.

"Don't be offended, Querida. Sig always got the attention for both of us. Turn to the back of the book. She was with me in the outdoor shot at Big Sur."

Ramona stopped her at a page that held a single eight by ten glossy. It was the only color shot I had seen. Marisol obviously hadn't seen it before. If her jaw had dropped any farther, it would have bounced off the coffee table.

The two women sat posed on boulders; half facing each other, framed by an arching madrona with the white capped Pacific Ocean for backdrop. There were only hairstyles and the fading of decades to establish that it had been taken in the 1940's. Sigrid Helstrom had lowered a leg just far enough to show that she was either naturally blonde or very meticulous in her bleach jobs. Ramona's pose was an open invitation. A daring ploy in its day, it was too redundant now to keep my eyes from Sigrid.

Just looking at a half-century old photograph of her, and even knowing she was really Cynthia Louise Halston from the east side of nowhere, I could still hear Wagner's *Ride Of The Valkyrie.*

"Sig was the one who made it, of course," Ramona said. "Nordic blondes were big in those days. Sig was pretty big herself, as you can see, in just the right places. She got her foot in the door, and I got to go along for the ride."

"Whom did she meet?"

"Malcolm Trevor." Ramona was an ingenue again, breathing the name of a heartthrob. "He was a genius."

"Was there ever a marriage?"

Ramona gave me a pitying smile. "What are you looking for, Mr. Spain? If you'd quit beating around the bush, I could probably tell you what you want to know. There wasn't much in Sig's life then that I wasn't part of."

"Her family would like to know if there is anything in her background that could qualify as a scandal."

Ramona glanced at her granddaughter and let out a thin, dancing laugh. "There's an expense you can save yourself, Querida. Just take your fingers out of your ears when I tell you about the fun I had when I was your age."

Marisol closed the photo album. "Gram, you make that up. You know you do."

Ramona teased me with her eyes. "What do you think, Mr. Spain? Am I just an over-the-hill broad craving attention?"

"Did Sigrid ever marry Trevor?"

"No one ever married Malcolm. He wasn't like most men when it came to women."

"Is that a nice way of saying he liked boys better than girls?"

Ramona laughed again, a fluttering giggle full of secret knowledge. "You young people get more innocent by the generation."

"Why don't you tell me about it? I think I'm old enough now."

"Malcolm was paranoid about any woman seeing him without his clothes on. Sig once told me she'd never seen him with his shirt off."

"Then there was no physical relationship?"

"Not in the Victorian sense of male penetration. The only way Malcolm could bring himself to climax was if he could see a woman doing herself. Except he had a polite way to put it. In the throes of erotic transport."

"That sounds like it could grow into something spicy. Did Sigrid ever go into details?"

"The girls always go into details, Mr. Spain. Half the fun is reliving it afterward."

"Do you think you could share any of it?"

"Malcolm would get undressed and get into bed. When he was ready, he would call Sig. She would come in nude and go to work on herself on a beautiful velvet couch he kept in the bedroom. That way he could do his business under the covers."

"Gram," Marisol scolded. "You don't know that's true. Even if your friend told you. You weren't there."

"The hell I wasn't, Querida. Your frail old grand-mother had to fill in for Sig once."

Marisol sucked half the air out of the room and turned flaming scarlet.

Ramona patted her hand again. "It was the height of my love life, Querida. New Year's Eve, 1951."

"Gram, stop."

"You see, Querida, there are men and then there are men. The Malcolm Trevors of this world are rare enough that you probably won't ever meet one. Those few minutes his eyes were devouring my body were the only time I ever had his full attention. I couldn't begin to tell you how it felt. The height of my love life, and he never put a hand on me."

"Did Granddad know?" Marisol was seized by a sudden, horrified hush.

"Your grandfather was the steady, reliable half of the man every woman is looking for. He was realistic enough to know that, and smart enough not to ask questions he didn't want to hear the answers to."

Marisol looked at me fearfully, as if she could already see her grandmother's picture on the cover of a supermarket tabloid. "Gram isn't that kind of person. It was that Sigrid. She must have been a bad influence."

"Sig was a lousy influence," Ramona told me. "But she paid the dues for both of us." Remorse shone like tears in her dark eyes.

"In what way?"

"It wasn't all naughty little games, Mr. Spain. Sig was raped. Gang banged, they called it back then."

"They still do. Do you know the circumstances?"

"There was no publicity, if that's what you're worried about. It happened at The Shadows. Things that happened there didn't wind up in the newspapers."

"The Shadows being—?"

"A nightclub. Mickey Cohen was supposed to be a silent partner. You do know who he was?"

Passing years and pulp novels had inflated Mickey Cohen into the bogeyman. The real Cohen had been a volatile bantam rooster who wore press coverage like elevator shoes. His fortunes and his power had fluctuated wildly during his years in the spotlight.

"When was Sigrid raped?"

"New Year's Eve, 1944. Mickey Cohen wasn't involved, of course. He probably never knew it happened."

"What did happen?"

"She was taken into a back office and used by five Army officers, one right after the other."

It sounded like a typical Sigrid Helstrom film role. "Were you in *Ambush Road*?" I asked with more than a little suspicion.

"The critics loved Sig in that one. It was her favorite. She kept the script. She practically destroyed it; she read it so many times."

"What is Malcolm Trevor doing these days?" I asked, hoping to find a slightly steadier witness.

"The Good Lord took him." Ramona tugged a lace handkerchief from her sleeve and dabbed at her eyes. "My bones weren't so porous then as they are now, and I was able to go to the service. The three flower petals I took away have turned to dust, but I keep them anyway. In a little bottle."

"Sigrid must have had other admirers?"

"Malcolm didn't allow that. He had Sig followed to make sure she didn't run around on him."

"Followed by whom?"

"Gabriel Skidmore."

I wrote the name. "Who was he?"

"A peeping tom from studio security," she said with a disgusted sniffle.

I zipped my portfolio and stood. It was definitely time to leave. Ramona was settling in for a good cry.

"Forgive me, Mr. Spain. God has taken my friends and my strength and the doctor said soon he will take me."

It was a nice touch to wrap up an Academy Award performance. She had seen me too willingly and shared her scandals too freely. I was supposed to think I had all the dirt on Sigrid Helstrom. I wasn't supposed to dig any deeper.

Marisol moved into the seat beside Ramona and put an arm around her shoulders. "We'll all miss you, Gram, but you'll be with Grand-dad." When that didn't help, she added, "And your friend, Sig."

"No Sig, Querida. Mis pecados no son mortales."

The phrase stopped me halfway to the door. "Were Sigrid's sins mortal?"

"Sig is gone!" Ramona said with a violence I would have thought beyond her strength. "Can't you let the poor creature sleep in peace?"

Her crying descended into racking sobs that threatened to shake her apart. I left before Marisol made something physical out of the murder in her eyes.

The video rental companies didn't stock *Ambush Road*, so I had to buy a copy off a retailer's bargain rack. The Investigators' Association listed a Gabriel Skidmore among its retired members. He answered his phone on the second ring. He might have time to see me tomorrow, if I would be so good as to tell him what I wanted. I told him I had a background assignment on someone he knew from his days at the studio, and that I would pay for his help.

Sigrid Helstrom had turned her meal ticket over to a super-heated Latina on the biggest party night of 1951. The same Sigrid Helstrom who would never see her friend in the hereafter because she had an undisclosed count of mortal sins against her soul. I hoped Malcolm Trevor had been as suspicious then as I was now, and that he had sent Gabriel Skidmore to follow Sigrid.

CHAPTER 5

Wiry, white haired and African American, Gabriel Skidmore answered his doorbell in khakis and brown loafers. He didn't seem to have noticed that South Central L.A. had changed into colorful sweats and sneakers.

"Good morning, Mr. Spain. Please come in."

I stepped into a shallow parlor with the Spartan look of life-long bachelorhood. Framed photographs filled the walls. Not the usual family portraits, they ranged from black and white shots of military life to color poses with backgrounds that might have been a movie lot.

"Quite a collection," I remarked, mostly to start him talking.

"I learned photography in the Army Public Information Office during World War II. I kept it up as a hobby when I joined studio security."

He installed me in a worn easy chair and, when I had declined coffee, settled himself in a thinly padded rocker.

"I seldom hear from my profession any more."

His words sent a chill up my spine. Never mind the difference in skin color. I was looking at myself in fewer years than I cared to think about. I wouldn't be hearing from anyone, either.

"You must have had your moments," I said, "working for Malcolm Trevor."

"I worked for the studio, Mr. Spain. My hours were billed to Mr. Trevor's budget on the occasions when he had assignments for me."

It seemed important to him that I understood that. Details mattered to men in our line of work. I decided my best approach was direct, one professional to another.

"One of those assignments was surveillance of an actress named Sigrid Helstrom."

"I can't imagine who might have told you that."

"Ramona Benitez."

Memories flickered in his eyes.

"Sigrid Helstrom's family retained me," I volunteered to assure him any secrets were safe.

"I suppose I could review my surveillance notes, if you'll tell me what you're looking for."

"The night I'm interested in is New Year's Eve, 1951."

He knew what I was talking about. That much was obvious from the troubled silence that settled over him.

"Trevor had you follow Sigrid."

His wordless acceptance made my guess a fact.

"She had turned him over to Ramona for the night."

"How much did Ramona know?"

The worry in Skidmore's question seemed out of place. As a former investigator, he would know that the statute of limitations had long since run out on anything that had happened in 1951. Anything except murder.

"We're talking about a serious matter, Mr. Skidmore. What can you tell me?"

"That surveillance was undertaken in confidence."

"Trevor is beyond caring."

"My obligation is good for my lifetime. Not his."

"Mr. Skidmore, I know how important loyalty to a client is, but the truth will come out. It might be best if it came from someone sympathetic to the people involved."

"Are you sympathetic, Mr. Spain?"

"I'm reserving judgment. I have some facts, but I don't think I have them all."

Maybe he believed me a little. Probably not much. He let out the resigned sigh of a man who simply had carried his burden too long.

"I followed Miss Helstrom from the studio after work," he said, seeming to drift back in time as he spoke. "She went directly home to the apartment she shared with Ramona. Mr. Trevor arrived at seven. I knew his car. It was a Bentley Continental. Very rare and expensive."

I smiled, partly to let him know I was listening, but mostly to cover my surprise. I'd given him no time for research or invention. His recollection of events fifty years gone should have been hazy at best. New Year's Eve, 1951, had seared itself into his memory in vivid detail.

He began rocking. "The lights in the apartment went out shortly after Mr. Trevor and Ramona left. I knew the neighborhood from previous surveillance. There were no cars that didn't belong. At first I thought Miss Helstrom was taking a nap before either going out or entertaining, but midnight came and passed. I was about to go home when her lights came on. Forty five minutes later she was picked up by a slim gentleman in a two tone blue Chrysler. Part way out Sunset, he slowed and flashed his lights twice. A dirty green Hudson with three men inside pulled out of a Flying A station and fell in behind the Chrysler."

It sounded like a re-run of New Year's Eve, 1944. If Skidmore knew about that, he didn't mention it.

"I was driving a ten year old Studebaker. I was afraid I wouldn't be able to keep up when they turned north on the Coast Highway. My motor was nearly overheated when we got to Delgado Bay."

I tried to remember whether I'd heard of the place. The fact that I couldn't probably showed on my face.

"It's just a cluster of quaint buildings today," Skidmore explained, "but it was a hot spot in the early 1950's. The Delgado Inn specialized in honeymoon suites for bachelors. Miss Helstrom kept watch while one of the men from the Hudson hot-wired the Inn's eight passenger DeSoto. The other two put on coveralls. The man who drove the Chrysler transferred a Carbine from the trunk of his car to the front seat of the DeSoto."

"When you say Carbine, do you mean a military M-2? An automatic rifle?"

He gave me a satisfied smile, like I had passed some secret test. "The DeSoto was known at the Caliente Beach Club. That was the key to their plan."

"Fill me in on the Caliente Beach Club." I tried to sound like I knew generally what he was talking about, but was a little fuzzy on the specifics.

"A metaphor for life. A place that existed solely for people to spend money they didn't have to impress people they didn't like."

I didn't need voice-over from *Lux Radio Theater*. "Can you give me a physical description?"

"A rambling building with picture windows that looked out toward the beach. I had been there before—following people from the studio because other people with more influence wanted to know how and where they wasted their money, and with whom—so I knew a secluded spot to park and watch."

I had an idea what was coming next. I could feel my fingers dig into the upholstery of the armchair. The tempo of Skidmore's rocking picked up.

"It was past closing when we arrived. The parking lot was nearly empty. The DeSoto stopped near the rear service door of the building. The driver remained inside. The others got out. The two men in coveralls went to the trash cans against the rear wall. Miss Helstrom and the slim man stood under a light at the corner of the building. When a yellow Oldsmobile turned down from the highway, they began to act like a party girl and her john."

"Who was in the car?"

"The passenger was a collector for Mickey Cohen. I saw him clearly when he went in the service door. I had seen him before, on the studio lot. Gangsters were attracted by the glamour of film studios. They made no secret of whom or what they were. It allowed them to swagger. To be part of the show."

"What about the driver?"

"He stayed in the car, kept the motor running. Miss Helstrom and the slim gentleman sauntered toward the DeSoto. They paused in front of the Oldsmobile for a romantic clinch. The collector came out with a heavy satchel and opened the trunk of the Oldsmobile. He was shot immediately, more than once. The two men in coveralls had worked their way to almost point blank range. Before the driver could react, Miss Helstrom and the slim gentleman shot him through the windshield."

"Sigrid did some of the shooting?"

Skidmore just nodded and went on. "The DeSoto pulled up beside the Oldsmobile. The slim gentleman recovered the Carbine. He fired a warning burst through the service door while the men in coveralls transferred satchels from the trunk of the Oldsmobile to the rear passenger area of the DeSoto. Miss Helstrom and the men piled in and they were gone. It all took less than a minute. I didn't dare follow. They would have been alert for any pursuit."

"What did you do?"

"Next morning I reported what I had seen to Mr. Trevor. He instructed me never to tell anyone."

Skidmore stopped rocking and settled back; a man finally at peace with his past. I put disappointment into my voice.

"I'll need to see your surveillance notes."

"Excuse me?"

"Your surveillance notes. To find out what really went on that night. What you just fed me was a scene from an old movie called *Ambush Road.* I watched it last night on the VCR. Sigrid Helstrom was a cast member."

Skidmore wasn't spry, but he got up with a little effort, left the room and returned with a brittle cardboard folder and a faded steno notebook. Contemporary news clippings backed up his story, right down to a photo of the bullet-riddled Oldsmobile. His surveillance notes were part of an unrelated chronological sequence and they gave the same account.

"You could have been a hero," I said, "reporting this to the police."

"I was a Negro. Following a white actress. In those days that would have been a greater scandal than the robbery."

"Do you know what was behind the robbery?"

"The Caliente Beach Club was probably the last stop on a pick up run that included Mickey Cohen's biggest night spots. The haul could have been hundreds of thousands."

I was thinking about Sigrid Helstrom, raped in another Cohen joint seven years earlier, her dog-eared script of *Ambush Road* under her arm, looking for payback. I also had an idea what was troubling Skidmore.

"It was pretty careless of Cohen's people, letting stick up artists learn their schedule."

A shrug was all he had to offer.

"You had seen the collector on the studio lot," I reminded him. "Maybe he was there to see Ramona."

He looked down at his shoes, a look that in a man with less pride might have been defeat. "Ramona was free spirited. It was natural for her, I suppose, to see a fling with a hoodlum as something daring and rebellious."

"Or as a source of information to plan a robbery."

He didn't say anything.

"You didn't go to the police because you were afraid Ramona fingered the robbery."

"Did she?" A fearful whisper, almost inaudible.

"I have her address, if you want to ask her."

He shook his head.

I didn't know what Ramona had been to him, or what she was now. Perhaps just a dream, safe and remote, with which he could fill his golden years. But I could see in his face it wasn't something he was going to risk with no guarantee that a visit to the real Ramona would put something of equal or greater value in its place. He wouldn't take any money, so I thanked him and left him alone with his memories.

I was suspicious of people who gave up their secrets as easily as Ramona and Skidmore had, but I had a glimmer of motive now. Fingering the Caliente Beach Club had probably been the most exciting thing that ever happened to Ramona. It was also a one-way ticket to the Big Adios if word got out. So she kept shut all these years. But now, looking into her own grave with nothing but a short legacy of b-movie credits to leave behind, she could finally let the world know how naughty she'd really been in her wayward youth. She aimed me at Skidmore, gambling, or perhaps knowing, that he'd followed Sigrid and knew the truth.

Skidmore was another track from the same CD. When the big one came along, a combination of loyalty to Trevor, racial injustice and infatuation with Ramona had curbed his tongue. Passing years had relegated the events to history, but they were all he had so he passed them on to me to keep alive after he was gone.

I would need corroboration to sell the story to Peter Lomax and his attorney wife.

I couldn't just stop by the library. The L.A. underworld of the forties and early fifties wasn't the sort of social phenomenon that attracted serious historians. It was the province of a few warped souls who got a vicarious charge from ferreting it out of old court records and period news publications. And even fewer surviving participants. I had the misfortune of knowing one of each.

The former was a title insurance lawyer. I was as close to actual crime as he would ever get, which wasn't very close. Normally I called him only when I was desperate for information from his company's ownership and tax records. Any contact doomed me to at least half an hour of listening to the latest installment of how things were in the bad old days. I dug out the cellular and got a surprise. He wasn't giving out information on the phone. I would have to meet him in person.

Chapter 6

My crime buff's choice for lunch was a downtown Teriyaki storefront already filling with corporate climbers in power ties and underwire bras. I appropriated the last of the minuscule tables and buried my nose in a discarded newspaper to wait.

The Aguilar killing was at the top of the police blotter. That probably meant the Spanish language media had picked up the story and the mainstream fish wrapper was regurgitating it to avoid accusations of insensitivity to a major market. It definitely meant pressure on law enforcement.

Putting the article together with what I knew, Aguilar had taken a work break half an hour before Stevie arrived in the late Harold Lomax's Bentley. I had been half a block away and hadn't heard the shot. Apparently no one else had either. If she hadn't come along, the body would have gone undiscovered until shift change and I would have gone home fat, dumb and happy. Instead of winding up as a deer in the headlights of an onrushing homicide investigation. So far I hadn't found Stevie to ask her what she was doing there.

Instead, Peter Lomax found me. According to Peter, daddy Harold was too old to play with girls Stevie's age. Peter wanted me to investigate his late mother's glory days as actress Sigrid Helstrom to protect his wife's upcoming political campaign. My information to date was that mama Cynthia had been up to her filmable assets in Class A felonies.

"Henry!"

The loud voice belonged to my crime buff. He balanced his bulk on a small chair and gave me a critical wag of his finger.

"I knew I'd hear from you eventually."

I folded the newspaper and stuck it under my chair. "Do you know an attorney named Mrs. Peter Lomax?"

"Paige? Not personally, my dear Sheerluck. We don't move in the same circles."

"Then she is prominent?"

"Becoming prominent," he corrected with a lawyer's love of nit picking. "Grooming herself to run for the City Council, if the gossip making the rounds in legal circles has any merit, which it occasionally does."

So much for Peter's confidential information. "Do you know anything about the family?"

"What are you fishing for, Henry?"

"Just checking. I've been offered a small assignment."

His eyes lit up. "Software piracy?"

I shook my head, but I remembered Lomax had bent my ear on the subject. "What exactly does Peter do at Prescott?"

"Vice President. Operations." He gave me a suspicious look. "Are you sure this isn't about software piracy?"

"Think about it," I ordered. "Would you hire a Neanderthal like me to ferret out high-tech evil doers? I wouldn't know what to look for."

"It's simple. There are only four flavors. The stuff you and I do; loading from someone else's CD-ROM. The commercial version of that; computer manufacturers loading software on new machines without paying the royalty. The big casino is replication; knocking off CD-ROMS from a master for the packaged goods market. And unauthorized discounting."

That was already more than I wanted to know, and judging from his eager expression he was just warming up.

He raised his water in a mock toast. "Breathes there a soul so indignant as the thief who finds himself robbed?"

"Lomax?" I asked.

"The industry, Henry. How do you stay so ignorant?"

"Diligence. Motivation. Natural aptitude."

Sarcasm didn't even slow him down. "The basic personal computer concepts were dreamed up at Xerox's Palo Alto Research Center in the seventies. Today's titans got their start by helping themselves without paying a nickel. Now they scream rape if anyone pilfers so much as a byte of their precious intellectual property."

Enough was enough. "You said Paige Lomax was grooming herself. What does that mean?"

He abandoned software piracy with a reluctant sigh. "Aligning herself with various worthy causes. Organizing a family law clinic for single mothers. Pro Bono work in a high profile parole case. Anything for media exposure."

"What are her chances?"

"She has the backing of her firm, Berkut and Schroeder. Placing a former partner in government brings in customers. These are lean and hungry times in the legal profession."

A waitress arrived and he ordered a small chicken plate that was liable to leave him lean and hungry. I took the same thing in the largest size they had.

"It's my check, if you want to upgrade."

He shook his head. "Seriously, Henry, what is your secret for keeping fit?"

I had to laugh. "Any relation between my current condition and fitness is purely nonexistent."

"You're not a pound over weight."

Ten was closer to the truth. "I have irregular eating habits."

"You work out. Don't try to tell me you don't."

"You're better off signing up with a gym than asking a no-show like me about fitness."

"Gyms are so, well, obvious."

I grinned. "Should I be saying cherchez la femme or something like that?"

He squirmed on the little chair, like someone had sharpened it under his backside. "I'm the unromantic lump women cross off their lists after one dinner."

"Congratulations. That's farther than I usually get."

"She's ten years younger than I am, Henry. And she could do a lot better."

"How many kids does she have?"

"Two."

"Forget the gym. Cultivate a settled, family look."

He turned a painful shade of red and glanced at nearby diners. His voice fell to practically nothing. "She brought up the subject of intimate relations. She isn't interested in anything extramarital."

"Pumping yourself up into a *Playgirl* centerfold won't change that. Do you have her particulars written out?"

"Pardon me?"

"You do want her checked out, don't you?"

He took a minute to repair his composure. "Do you think I'm being foolish?"

"If she has another boyfriend, and she is doing the deed with him, it will do you no good to confront her with his identity. She will tell you she is not your property, which is true, and that she is not looking for a purely physical relationship, which is also true, or she wouldn't be seeing you on a platonic basis. If she marries you for security and stability, she will probably drop her outside interests and keep it in the family until she passes forty."

"Why forty?" The idea seemed to bother him more than my suggestion that the light of his life might be physically involved elsewhere.

"As they grow older, men become more conservative, women more radical. Forty is about the age when women start wishing they'd protested for peace and saved the environment and done it on the first date and all the other things they imagine they've missed."

"You've done too much domestic work," he said, and let the conversation lapse while the waitress set out chicken and rice.

The last wandering wife I'd located had given me the same impression. I found her on the Navajo Reservation, communing with nature to the amazement of several little boys who hadn't seen many naked women. She informed me that returning to her marriage was not conceptually relevant, since she was not really a person, but a form of love energy from another dimension. I wasn't sure what she meant when she offered to spread her aura. Since I never engaged in either sex or close combat with women who outweighed me, there was nothing to do but report back to her husband.

"Seriously," I said, trying to atone for my callous remarks, "there are capable women who make a career of this sort of investigation. Any one of them could give you a better fix on where your lady is coming from than I could."

He sprinkled soy sauce on his sparse lunch, and was flustered enough to garnish his tie as well. "I'm sorry, Henry. I thought I was ready to hire you. Now I find myself with an embarrassing case of cold feet. Or maybe I just owe myself a few more wet dreams before reality sets in."

"In between ejaculations, do you suppose you could tell me about the Caliente Beach Club?"

"I've never heard of it."

"It was one of Mickey Cohen's night spots. In Delgado Bay. Two of Cohen's collectors were robbed and murdered there on New Year's Eve, 1951."

"That was a fertile time for dastardly doings."

"I'm talking serious money. Hundreds of thousands."

"A feather in the breeze, Henry. The Mob shook down the film industry for more than a million during the depression, when a dollar was really worth something. Buggsy Seigel blew six million building the Flamingo Hotel in Vegas, and even that wouldn't have been news if his associates hadn't shot him dead as a result."

"All right, forget the money. Mickey Cohen had a reputation to protect. He had to retaliate."

"Honestly, how do you survive as an investigator?"

"What am I missing?"

"Have you ever heard of McNeil Island?"

"It was a Federal prison, wasn't it?" I had visions of a concrete fortress on a barren rock in Puget Sound, half obscured by the drizzle that had greeted me on my few trips to Seattle.

"Meyer Harris Cohen was sent there in November of 1951 for an extended period of meditation on the merits of scrupulous adherence to the Internal Revenue Codes."

His suggestion that a power vacuum made Cohen's empire vulnerable had some intuitive charm, but it wasn't the factual clincher I was looking for. We finished lunch and parted friends in spite of the short shrift I had given his romantic dilemma.

I had no friendship at stake in my second meeting. Terrence Llewelyn Stafford had made his bones as a foot soldier in the L.A. gambling wars that preceded the rise of Las Vegas in the early fifties. No one called him Tough Tommy any more, but the tailored suit and the affable manner just meant he gave orders now instead of taking them.

"I've been expecting your call," he said.

He absent-mindedly took out one of his long, green-dappled cigars and the last three months evaporated. I was back in the den of his Pasadena mansion where a collection of antique slot machines stared at me through their vacant eyes.

"Find Hamilton," Stafford had ordered, smoke leaking from his nostrils as he set me on the trail of a dead man.

Guy Hamilton was a hack talent agent, a bottom feeder who wound up on the bottom of Catalina Channel when he accidentally learned that an L.A. urban legend was true. The story went that for years players in the power structure laundered questionable money by purchasing real estate in the names of dead people. Whoever held the list that matched the names to the real estate controlled a shadow empire now worth untold millions. When the list surfaced, Hamilton caught three bullets trying to cash in. The warped accountant who followed him stopped four. The list was as toxic as a vial of anthrax, and I was next in the chain of possession.

Stafford hadn't hired me for a simple skip-trace. He wanted the list. If I gave it up, he'd kill me to buy silence. If I refused, he'd kill me to keep it away from his adversaries. If I went to the authorities, I exposed myself to the players in the original scheme. I had enough trouble with day to day decisions. Impossible dilemmas were well beyond my limited capacity. The best idea I could come up with was to keep the list as life insurance and give him one property at a time, hoping the uncollected rent and unpaid taxes on the properties he didn't get would arouse enough suspicion that the empire would collapse under its own weight before he could consolidate it. He had fired up another of his cigars while he weighed his risks against his dreams.

The image faded as Stafford remembered where he was and put the finely crafted tobacco back in his pocket. This was the lobby of the downtown Sheraton. Nobody smoked here. Or committed murder either.

He sank into a gondola chair with far less effort than his seventy odd years should have required and left me alone with my thoughts while his eyes devoured the sheet of computer print-out I'd handed him. I sat down and waited until his expression told me he realized how juicy a plum it was.

"I want a bonus," I said.

He lifted his eyebrows. "Not money," he decided.

"I want to know who took down the Caliente Beach Club on New Years Eve, 1951."

He folded the printout and tucked it into an inner pocket. "Why?" he asked, too casually.

"What difference can it make at this late date?"

"You've heard of The Night of the Sicilian Vespers?"

I shook my head.

"In the first third of the last century, the Mafia in this country was run by immigrant Sicilian bosses. Younger, American-born members resented that. In September, 1931, they killed forty one of the old timers and took over. They used outsiders to do the killing. Jew guns like Ben Siegel. The old Mafia survivors resented that. Power struggles were a fact of life, but you were supposed to keep them in the family."

"Was Mickey Cohen involved?"

His shrug told me it didn't matter. "The worry was that descendants of the old Mafia had recruited their own outside guns to reclaim power."

"Twenty years later?"

"We're talking Italian organized crime. Grudges are passed down from generation to generation."

"Then nobody really knew who took down the Beach Club?"

"Only that it was the second Cohen club taken down in three years. Both on New Year's eve."

I tried out another scene from *Ambush Road.* "The manager of The Shadows brought the New Years Eve receipts out the back door. He was disabled by a shotgun blast then executed with a handgun. The club was torched."

Stafford's scrutiny told me I was right. "What's it about?"

He almost certainly was probing for chinks in my armor, for any sign of trouble he could hold over me. I thanked him for the information and drove to my office to call Peter Lomax.

"Something has come up in your mother's background. I need to talk to you and your wife as soon as possible."

"You may report your findings to me. I'll check my calendar."

"I'm afraid it won't wait, Mr. Lomax. Your mother's activities involved more than just titillating scandal."

"Specifically what?" He sounded dubious.

"Two counts of armed robbery and three of murder."

"Nonsense."

"One count of arson. One count of accessory to grand theft auto. One count of carrying a concealed weapon. One count of accessory to possession of an unregistered automatic weapon."

"Mr. Spain—" he tried to interrupt.

"Indecent exposure, numerous acts of moral turpitude—Mr. Lomax, I think you and your wife and I should talk."

I was tired of the charade. It was time to drop the Lomax family mess back in their laps, find out what kind of games daddy Harold had played with Stevie and what, if anything, they had to do with the shooting of a medical student in East L.A.

Lomax gave me driving directions to his home, and we agreed on seven o'clock.

CHAPTER 7

Highland Avenue north of Wilshire was the western boundary of Hancock Park, a neighborhood of stately homes that had started life with huge Pierce Arrows in garages that now held the latest in overgrown SUVs. My personal car was an old Porsche 912E that screamed mid-life crisis to a world that couldn't care less. I parked it in the Lomax's driveway.

Ground level lamps lit my way to the front door where a luminous button waited to announce me to a loftier stratum of society. Muted chimes rang briefly in the house. A chilly breeze rustled a nearby hedge. It seemed like I had spent my life standing out in the cold waiting for someone who never came to let me in.

Before I could put my finger back on the button, the door opened. Peter Lomax had traded his business sport coat for umpteen dollars worth of gentleman's tweed.

"Come in, Mr. Spain," he said in a voice that barely tolerated my existence, let alone my presence in his home.

The entry was formal and angular in design, but that hadn't fazed the decorator. Indirect lighting shimmered through blown-glass artwork in a rainbow of pastel colors. Hypnotic swirls of silver flowed through the ribbed ochre carpet. An arid fragrance filled the air. I had never been in a French whorehouse, but this place reminded me of one anyway.

Lomax led me along a hall and ushered me into a library. The light there came from ornate lamps strategically placed to emphasize more glasswork and banish the bookshelves of a bygone generation to the shadows.

"Mr. Spain, my wife, Paige."

She put aside a blue-backed document and came out of her chair with the quickness of a raptor. She was as tall as Peter, lean and angular in flowery harem trousers and a silk blouse. Her handshake felt like the talons of a falcon picking off a sparrow for dinner.

"I inquired about you today, Mr. Spain. Or tried to. I couldn't find anyone in the legal community who was familiar with your work."

"Litigation support is outside my scope."

She smiled as if she couldn't imagine what other legitimate work there might be for an investigator, but would give me the benefit of any doubt, no matter how skimpy. "Perhaps you have references you would like to present?"

"Mrs. Lomax, I'm not here to apply for an assignment. I'm here to disengage myself from one. While I am licensed for general investigative work, my specialty is skip tracing. I think, after reviewing my report, you'll agree that is not what your situation calls for."

I gave them each a copy. We sat down and I went through the adventures of the late Cynthia Louise Lomax, felony by felony.

"This," Peter declared when I finished, "is just the sort of slander you were retained to discredit."

I was reminding him about the contemporary news accounts when music started up somewhere else in the house, low and syncopated. Paige was on her feet instantly. She marched to a wall intercom.

"Cynthia, I would like that television off right now, please. You have homework."

"But Mom," came a whiny voice, "it's my favorite group. They're only on MTV once this—"

"Cynthia."

A defeated, "Yes, Mother," came from the speaker.

The television cut off. Paige sat down again.

"My husband's mother fell in with the wrong crowd when she was young. Is that the substance of your report?"

"The facts suggest otherwise."

"Explain."

"The robberies were committed according to the script of Sigrid Helstrom's favorite film. The first club targeted was the place where she was gang raped. It was taken down on the anniversary of her rape. The second club was also taken down on the anniversary of her rape. She organized both as a way of striking back."

"You have no proof."

"I want none."

Paige arched her eyebrows at me. "What sort of attitude is that?"

"Your husband asked me to investigate his mother's background for potential embarrassment to your upcoming political campaign. I think this qualifies."

She scowled at the mention of her ambitions. "I want these incidents taken apart, Mr. Spain. I want to know to a certainty what really happened. Names. Dates. Witnesses. Everything."

"Anything I find will have to go to the police."

"It will not," she said with the assurance of superior knowledge. "I am the attorney of record for the Estate of Cynthia Louise Lomax, nee Halston, AKA Sigrid Helstrom. I am responsible to keep myself apprised of potential claims against the estate, such as might arise from alleged criminal activity. The findings of any investigation conducted in pursuit of my duties are privileged."

I had called this meeting to bail out of my assignment, but the fact was that I had stumbled onto a witness to two murders and hadn't run straight to the police with the news. It was probably a long shot, but the wrong kind of backlash could cost me my license. As much as I disliked the idea, Paige's attorney-client privilege would make a good hiding place if the issue ever came up.

"Will you provide me an engagement letter to that effect?"

"Of course."

"The only reference I can offer on short notice is Jerry Freegate, the auto dealer."

"Mr. Freegate is a long-standing Berkut and Schroeder client. I'll call him tomorrow."

That bit of coincidence bothered me, but I let it pass. "I will need the details of the relationship between your father-in-law and Stephanie St. John."

Anger flushed Peter's face and brought him to his feet in a sudden lurch. Large, soft men often saw their physical size as intimidating. Looming over me was probably his idea of a threat.

"The relationship, and that is stretching the word, consisted of a young woman taking advantage of a man nearing the end of his capacity to reason effectively."

"You hired me to investigate your mother to keep me busy so I wouldn't check on your father and Stephanie St. John. What did you think I might find?"

He got as far as, "Now you look here, Spain," before Paige's laugh silenced him. She couldn't have chilled me any more effectively if she had touched an ice cube to my spine.

"Mr. Spain," she said, rolling my name around on her tongue as if she weren't sure she liked the taste of it, "do not read too much into your encounter with Ms. St John. She is what is politely termed an adventuress."

"Our encounter involved finding a murdered medical student."

"I'm well aware of the circumstances. I spoke to the police when they called."

"They called you because Ms. St. John was driving your late father-in-law's Bentley."

"I'm aware of the circumstances," she repeated in a tone that told me the subject was closed.

"You knew Stephanie St. John was driving a Bentley belonging to the Lomax estate?"

"We hadn't repossessed the car simply because we didn't know where it was."

"It doesn't sound right, Mrs. Lomax. Letting a six figure asset go missing without reporting it to the police."

"I don't think I like the implication, Mr. Spain."

"You also may not like what my investigation turns up. The Caliente Beach Club was a risky venture. If things didn't go exactly right, the gang could have been shot dead by their intended victims. The participants had to be professionals, including your mother in law. That means she had a prior history of armed robbery."

"Just find the facts, Mr. Spain. Let me deal with them." She went back to her reading and left Peter to show me out.

I watched for a tail when I backed out of the driveway. Paige didn't strike me as the trusting type. I had given Peter notice of what I would be delivering. Paige had plenty of time to arrange for surveillance. I wasn't sure what to make of the BMW parked down the street.

It was an older three series coupe, the kind of car driven by stockroom clerks who wanted to look trendier than their jobs. It had seen better days, and definitely didn't belong on Highland Avenue. It was also well below the talent Paige could afford. Maybe it was just some high school hormone stalking a cheerleader.

The driver hunkered down behind the wheel as I rolled by reading his license number into my recorder. All I saw was a stocking cap. I motored down Highland with one eye on the mirror.

The guy in the BMW had seen too many re-runs of *The Rockford Files*. The key to establishing a tail was to start accelerating as soon as your quarry passed. That took his speed advantage into account, gave you less than a one-block separation almost every time and made you look like nothing more than a polite motorist waiting your turn to pull into traffic. Stalling until the mark was a block past then snapping on the high beams and lighting the tires to catch up was far enough below amateur to suggest a two digit IQ and violent tendencies. I had a vision of the Porsche crumpled against a light pole, riddled by automatic gunfire, with me slumped behind the wheel leaking blood all over the upholstery. I made speed to Wilshire, hoping the busy boulevard would discourage felonious behavior.

The BMW was still trying to close up as the traffic took us through MacArthur Park. An intersection light stopped it. I took the ramp for the Harbor Freeway, got off at the first exit and wound through a maze of surface streets watching front, back and both sides. The BMW might have been a plant to distract me from a front tail or a parallel job. Twenty blocks of nothing eliminated that possibility, so I headed for my home in the Valley confident that I had put my troubles behind me for the evening.

An unfamiliar mini-van was waiting in my driveway. The lights were out and the driver was a dark shape.

CHAPTER 8

The minivan was parked with its nose pointed at the garage door. I slowed and used the remote. The door segmented up. Light from inside hit the minivan's windshield and illuminated the startled driver. It was Cassandra Freegate. My heart rate started back down, but my curiosity meter pegged. I pulled past her into the garage and climbed out to learn what had brought her.

It didn't seem to be a dress-up occasion. Her hair was pulled back into a ponytail and her windbreaker looked like she had charmed it off a high school letterman. She came into the garage with a nervous smile.

"The house was dark. I thought it would be okay to wait." She had a low, vibrant voice that would make anything okay.

My rec room wasn't Pacific Palisades. The pool table was closer to second hand than antique and the rectangular lamp suspended above it came from Coca-Cola, not Tiffany.

"What do you drink?" I asked.

"Scotch would be nice."

I measured a polite ounce over ice then mixed myself a stiff Cuba Libre to wash out the taste of the Lomax family. Daddy Harold who ran out into traffic and left Stevie St. John driving his Bentley. Mama Cynthia who rode in the Bentley of a man who watched her do herself on a velvet couch and kept the hired help quiet when she got trigger happy. Son Peter who didn't want to see mama as anything but mama and daughter-in-law Paige who saw her only as a speed bump on the road to power and prominence. To hell with them. It would be a relief talking to a normal wife and mother.

Cassandra toured the room with restless grace, inspecting the decor as if she needed time to work up her nerve. "You live alone," she decided.

"Yes."

She shrugged out of her windbreaker and tossed it over the back of the sofa. Slipping out of a pair of flat-heeled shoes, she curled up on the cushions at one end. In chinos and a man's flannel shirt, she didn't look much like Pacific Palisades herself. I gave her the drink and settled at the other end of the sofa, away from temptation. She was dangerous without even trying.

"Do you ever feel like you're rattling around in a place this size?"

"As a kid I never had a place to call home."

My old man never got along with his union, or anyone else for that matter. Jobs came and went and he shuttled the family from one cheap rental to another, always in the Hollenbeck district of Boyle Heights, where the Mexicans made more noise than he did and wouldn't dare call the cops on a gringo no matter how mean drunk he got.

Cassandra nibbled her scotch. "I rattle a lot. Sometimes I just have to drive, even if I don't have anywhere to go."

Velocity as an anesthetic was as a familiar concept. In my teens it had translated to a '57 Ford and the lyric of a rockabilly song that went something like: *Ninety miles an hour in a driving rain, if I was going any slower I would feel the pain.* I was lucky I hadn't wound up dead or in prison. Which reminded me of my trip into East L.A. to look for her son.

"Did the police call you?" I asked.

"Jerry talked to them."

"I hope he wasn't too upset." I didn't need a ticked off client on top of everything else.

"He was fascinated. I think it was the closest he had ever been to something really bad."

I wondered if it was the closest she had been. Something had worried her enough to bring her out to the Valley on a cold night and keep her waiting until I got home. She fortified her courage with a slug of scotch.

"Robbie's going to run again, isn't he?" She seemed resigned to the idea, just waiting for me to confirm it.

"I've never met Robbie," I reminded her.

"You knew where he ran to. I'm his mother, and I didn't have a clue."

I couldn't bring myself to confess that finding Robbie had been blind luck, so I ducked the issue with a modest shrug. "Any idea what he was running from?"

"My expectations?" she asked uneasily. "Or Jerry's? I don't know. I was hoping you could tell me. You deal with this sort of thing all the time."

"The general rule is that marijuana means anxiety," I said. "Kids who feel they are victims of expectations usually turn to alcohol."

"Seriously?" She sat up and paid attention.

Unfortunately, that was all I knew on that particular subject. "Have you thought about professional counseling?"

She made a face and went back to nibbling her drink. "Jerry and I have been through a couple of bouts of that. It didn't change the way I was. Just the way I pretended to be."

"Did it change Jerry?"

"It smoothed a few of his edges. Jerry is wound a couple of turns too tight, as you probably noticed, but he's basically a sentimental guy. I mean, the family cat started out as a stray kitten they found hiding in a parts bin at one of the dealerships."

"Have you talked to him about Robbie's adjustment problems?"

She swallowed the last of her scotch and got up to get her own refill. Her shirt filled when she ducked under the bar. I wondered how long the ice in my Cuba Libre would last.

I had been wrong about her taking ice in her scotch. She dumped the cubes into the sink, loaded her glass to the rim, flipped on the CD player, picked up the rhythm and swayed back to the sofa to sit shoulder to shoulder with me, staring across the room.

"Jerry spotted me in a chorus line in Vegas nine years ago. He came to a party after the show and I chilled him. Two days later he knocked on my apartment door with a dozen roses for me and a Nintendo game for Robbie. I made coffee and explained that I'd want both rings before we could even talk about him becoming part of my social life. That's a quick deflate for the male egos that show up in Vegas. They flip you off and you never hear from them again. Jerry just took off his coat and showed Robbie how to hook the Nintendo up to the TV. A month later he had me in front of a priest, and I'm not even Catholic. We're different, Mr. Spain, Jerry and me. We talk, but I'm not sure we communicate."

"It's Henry," I said.

"What do I say to him, Henry?"

"What kind of relationship do Jerry and Robbie have?"

"Robbie is the son Jerry always wanted and the doctors told him he could never conceive."

"And Robbie?"

"He's moody, withdrawn."

"How does Jerry feel about that?"

"It's a challenge for him. That's how Jerry sees life. As a series of challenges. I was a challenge. I was so terrified of the guy we were three days into our honeymoon before he got to second base with me."

"Is he physically abusive?"

"No, he's sweet. It's just that, well—where did you grow up?"

"Down by Hollenbeck Bridge."

"Was it a tough neighborhood?"

"We thought street fighting was an Olympic sport."

"But you wear a coat and tie now," she observed.

"When I have to."

"You've got one foot in the world you're in today and one still back in the world you grew up in."

Today was all I had left. The pachucos I'd grown up with were gone, claimed by Vietnam, street crime or prison. I took a stiff swallow of my Cuba Libre to send the memories back where they belonged.

"You're not really comfortable in either, are you?" she asked.

"I've made my choices."

"You're not married because it means committing to one world or the other, and you can't do that."

"Are you asking about me? Or trying to tell me about Robbie?"

"Kids pick up more than you'd think when they're little. Robbie's dad was a construction laborer. Robbie was six when he was killed in a fall. Jerry came along a year later and things changed overnight. Big time. The school, the kids, the values. Everything. It was too much, too fast for Robbie. He's smart enough to do well in the classes he likes, but he gravitates to the crowd that smokes and swears because they're the kind of people who were around when he was young."

"Where is he tonight?"

"Jerry took him to the Lakers' game."

"Jerry is your best shot," I said.

"Jerry is a lot of pressure for a sixteen year old."

"Count your blessings, Mrs. Freegate. Robbie is a choir boy compared to me at that age."

"It's Cassandra," she said.

"Cassandra."

"How did you make the adjustment?"

"Under duress," I said, wishing I hadn't brought up the subject.

It wasn't enough. She had come because she was worried about her son. She wanted to know what made young men tick. She wanted details. I could feel her breath on my face. My blood pressure was climbing. Talking was the only safety valve I had. I told her about coming back from Vietnam with no usable skills except some back alley locksmithing.

An investigator with a national agency caught me trying to drill a safe. He needed eyes on the street, and I didn't want to go to prison. At first I was an errand boy and a snitch. When the agency needed strikebreakers, I went on the payroll. From there I moved on to industrial espionage, felony bail jumpers, anything else they didn't want to send family men on.

"Now I'm a blue-collar cynic who took college courses back when he still thought he could get ahead in a white-collar world. You couldn't find a worse role model."

"I'm not looking for one," she said.

"What, then?"

"I don't know. Maybe just someone I can talk to without being clucked over or handed a lot of psycho-babble."

I put my arm on the back of the sofa, behind her shoulders. Her warmth and fragrance filled my head with ideas that didn't include conversation. She didn't object when I kissed her. I put my drink aside and kissed her again. Both kisses had more questions than passion in them. Neither of us had forgotten she was married.

"Would you like to go on with this?" I asked.

Her eyes filled with silent laughter. She probably had heard better lines in junior high school. Another swallow of scotch made her voice lower and more vibrant.

"Yes."

I led the way back to the bedroom with a stomach full of butterflies. The first thing she did was get rid of my coat and tie. I didn't try to undo any of her clothes. My own buttons were giving me enough trouble, partly because I was working by feel so I wouldn't miss anything while she undressed.

She seemed to enjoy the attention. She had no emotional investment in me, no memory bank of partner needs she had to satisfy. I was just a temporary link to a comfortable past.

There was nothing tentative when we came together. I buried my face in the softness of her breasts and teased her nipples with my tongue. She didn't object to my fingers sketching the outline of her pubic hair and moving inward from there. An electric thrill told me she was doing her own exploring.

When things swam back into focus there was only the romantic lilt of a CD down the hall and the silence of two strangers thrown together by chance. Cassandra broke it with a low, ironic laugh.

"Was I that amusing?" I asked.

"Not you. Roger Berkut. He told Jerry to use an established firm to find Robbie."

"Berkut being Jerry's lawyer?" Paige had told me Jerry was a Berkut and Schroeder client.

"His lawyer. His mentor. Roger was the first person who had any faith in Jerry. He was the first investor in the dealerships, and the one who negotiated the franchises with the manufacturers."

That made Jerry sound like a glorified salesman. "Why did your husband hire me?"

"Jerry has an impulsive streak. He heard your name from someone who was buying a car. That was all it took. It's just the way he is."

Cassandra wanted to get home before Jerry and Robbie did, so she was up and dressed and out the front door without a lot of conversation.

Standing in the doorway watching her minivan out of sight it dawned on me that Roger Berkut had been right. Jerry should have used an established firm to find Robbie. If he had, I wouldn't have been sitting in East L.A. when Eladio Aguilar was killed. I would never have learned about the high crimes and misdemeanors of Sigrid Helstrom. I wouldn't be hiding from the police behind Paige Lomax's attorney client privilege.

And I wouldn't be trying to locate a drop-dead blonde named Stevie St. John to find out how much trouble I gotten myself into trying to impress her.

CHAPTER 9

I spent the morning commute working out my campaign to locate Stevie only to get off the elevator and find her waiting outside my office. It was definitely a dress-up occasion. Her business suit tried for subdued elegance, but women who looked like Stevie didn't subdue. The old hallway lit up when she smiled.

"Good morning," she said in a husky voice that took me back to East L.A. "Remember me?"

"Somewhat," I managed to choke out through my surprise.

She gave me just enough room to unlock the door. In three-inch pumps her height matched mine. My nostrils filled with the fragrance of Shalimar and I knew Cassandra hadn't trimmed my horns down far enough.

My office was a one-bay remainder furnished in what a less critical visitor had called eclectic. I installed Stevie in a reupholstered art deco client chair and sat behind the desk to try for a little professional composure.

"I appreciate your stopping by, Stevie. I'd like to compare notes on our police interviews."

"They thought you were working for me. They asked if I checked your background before I hired you. Like you were dangerous or something."

My harmless grin came automatically, and felt slightly foolish. "I'm a skip tracer, Stevie. Runaway children, fugitive debtors, the occasional reluctant witness—anything but bail jumpers."

"Could you find out who killed my dad?"

She hadn't come to talk about East L.A. She had come to hire me. The police had probably asked her some questions based on the contents of my file and left her with an exaggerated idea of who and what I was.

"Stevie, I'm not a criminal investigator." The agency had discovered I was easily distracted by petty issues like the truth and decided my talents lay elsewhere.

"Do you know what a Starliner is?"

Enright had asked me a variation of the same question. I shook my head and tried not to look curious.

"It was the last of the long range piston airliners. They weighed over seventy tons. The engines were turbo-charged twenty-eight cylinder compound radials with fully reversing propellers. A good pilot could stop one on a twenty five hundred foot strip at full—"

"Give me a break, Stevie. I can recognize an aisle seat two tries out of three."

"My dad was a good pilot. He flew nineteen years without an accident."

"The police said you were a commercial pilot."

"Flight instructor," she corrected.

She was all business now. The vamp routine had just been a way to get her foot in the door. It occurred to me that I might not be the first target of that approach.

"Stevie, does this have anything to do with Harold Lomax?"

Her jaw tightened. "He was stationed at the Embassy in Saigon."

Lomax's obituary had put him there just before the city fell to the communists. "Was your father in Vietnam?"

"He was a contract pilot for Air America."

"Your father flew for the CIA?"

"He was based at a place called Bien Hoa."

My tour in Vietnam had taken me to Bien Hoa only once. I was going back up-country to my unit after R and R. Two hundred of us were crammed together on the metal floor of a C-130 cargo plane. We landed at Bien Hoa to drop some replacements. It wasn't a normal landing. The pilot braked hard as soon as he touched down then made a sharp turn off the runway. We bumped over pierced steel planking and stopped with the engines still turning. When the crew dropped the rear load gate we were in the middle of a storage area. It was night, and all I could make out at first were the dim shapes of palletized cargo. The signature crump of exploding mortar rounds told me the base was under attack.

The defensive wire was too far away to see directly, but the red arcs of tracer bullets showed the fight. The replacements got the message and wanted to evacuate the plane. It didn't work that way. The aircrew couldn't waste time collecting stray passengers from bunkers all over the base. Accidental losses were factored into that week's casualty estimates. Fresh meat was already in the pipeline. So we sat, spectators at the same thing we would be doing soon to stay alive, watching as two F-100's blasted down the runway and hauled wing-loads of napalm into the dark sky.

It was over in thirty minutes and we were airborne again, but it was so bizarre it had stayed with me ever since. And left me ready to believe almost anything I heard about Bien Hoa. Almost anything.

"Stevie, Vietnam was over before you were born."

"It's all in the book," she said, as if that settled everything.

"The book?"

"Harold Lomax tricked my father into flying contraband gold from Bien Hoa to California. A man named Alex Sturtevant wrote a book about it. That's how I found out what happened."

"This Alex Sturtevant—was he the man you were supposed to meet in East L.A?"

"We're going to see him this morning."

Just like that. Not even a 'Congratulations, you're hired.' I didn't argue. It was a chance to get the information I wanted, so I booted up the desk computer.

"I'll need your full name for the employment contract."

"Stephanie Anne St. John." She gave me an address in Beverly Hills, a phone number and a nervous smile. "We need to talk about money."

I told her my rate. She lost a little color.

"No one makes a living giving flying lessons," she said. "It's just something you have to do to work your way up to an airline job."

"What do you do for a living?"

"House sitter. Sales clerk. Department store model—mostly restaurant shows and Sunday supplements."

"Is that where you got the outfit?"

"Photo shoots ruin them for resale. They have to hook sash weights in back to get them to drape properly."

Between house sitting in Beverly Hills, modeling Rodeo Drive fashions and driving Harold Lomax's Bentley, Stevie was doing pretty well for someone with no money. It didn't take much intellectual horsepower to figure out that a first class hustler wouldn't be using her act on a marginal investigator if she weren't genuinely troubled about her father's death and running short of places to turn. I clicked *close* and *save* to put her contract on hold.

"Why don't we go see your Mr. Sturtevant? If I think I can help you, then we'll talk money."

I drove.

Stevie's directions took us east on Interstate 10. Traffic thinned as we rolled through the deeper suburbs of Claremont and Rancho Cucamonga. Drizzle washed some of the smog out of San Bernardino. The endless strip malls faded into agriculture. The Fontana rail yards drifted past, as vast and dingy as ever.

All the scenery added up to a long drive, and plenty of time for Stevie to tell me about her father's death. Stripped of emotional baggage, the story was pretty simple. When the conflict in Southeast Asia wound down, he found a job with an air freight company flying a four engine turboprop. One night his freighter slammed into a hangar during taxi operations. No one on board survived the resulting fire. The NTSB investigation blamed it on a mechanical failure called a propeller over-speed.

"It was sabotage," Stevie declared in a voice that expected me to prove it. "You better get in the right lane. I think we want the next exit."

The last cherry grove had fallen behind us. Drizzle was a memory. The air was as parched as the dun colored earth. We left the Interstate and found our way to two lanes of blacktop. The road wound through empty country where the government had offered five acre homesteads as late as the 1940's. Things that happened out here could go unnoticed for a long time. Maybe forever. I asked Stevie how much she really knew about this Alex Sturtevant character.

She had lost all desire for conversation. She was getting close to finding out what happened to her father. Which left me trying to keep my mind off her perfume and my eyes off her legs. I never saw where the pick-up truck came from.

One minute we were alone on the road, the next there was a green shape growing in the mirror. The hairs on the back of my neck stood up. Stevie noticed me watching the mirror and twisted in the seat to look back.

"Better give them room to pass."

There wasn't much room to give. A ravine had swallowed us. Rock walls rose steeply on either side, with only a couple of feet of dirt margin separating them from the blacktop. I eased to the edge of the pavement.

The truck filled the mirror. It was an older model, high-slung and dirty. The driver and passenger were both men, but their faces were above my roofline. I glanced to the side mirror. At the speed they were moving, I expected to catch sight of them immediately. When I didn't, I knew the driver had matched speed in my blind spot. Instinct yanked my foot off the accelerator.

The explosion went off almost in my ear. I had a glimpse of a gun barrel disappearing into the passenger's window as the truck rocketed past and accelerated away down the road. Washboard bumps warned me the right side tires had drifted onto the margin. I panicked and jerked on the wheel.

We were sliding in a heartbeat. The world started to spin. I held my breath and waited for impact. The Volvo did a three-sixty and wound up pointed in the direction we'd been going originally, but sitting at a dead stop in the wrong lane. I spent a confused minute wondering why the accelerator didn't get us moving.

"It's stalled," Stevie said as if I were a slow student in a flying lesson.

Her enforced calm covered an undercurrent of disbelief. I could still remember the feeling from when the first rifle rounds cracked over my head in Vietnam. It wasn't easy to accept the fact that someone hates you enough to want to kill you.

I could only guess why the two men in the GMC hadn't stayed around to finish the job. Maybe they were afraid I was armed. Maybe they were just plain scared. And maybe they'd get over their case of nerves and come back. I got the engine started and got us under way.

My next challenge was to collect my thoughts. It wasn't much of a collection. All I could remember of the truck were the grimy letters GMC spread across the tailgate.

"Did you get the license number?" I asked Stevie.

"Who were they?" she asked.

I hadn't seen the face of either man. "Who knew we were coming?"

"Just Alex Sturtevant."

"Who knew you were meeting him in East L.A. Friday?"

"Just him and me."

I let the Volvo pick up a little speed. My yen to meet the author had taken on a new urgency.

CHAPTER 10

Alex Sturtevant's address was a rural mailbox. A pair of ruts took us around a rise and up to a secluded knoll where concrete blocks supported a dusty trailer. I parked beside an old cream colored Jeep station wagon solely out of suburban habit. There was no driveway or yard. Just a random bit of flat area in the barren hills. We climbed two wooden stairs to a small porch and I knocked on the metal door.

The trailer oscillated under a heavy step. The door swung out a cautious foot then opened wide. Sturtevant had started out stocky and expanded horizontally over the years. Gray streaked a neatly trimmed beard and touched more lightly the hair receding over a tanned scalp. A buckskin pullover did its best to give him a rugged outdoor persona.

"You'd be Stephanie," he said in a fatherly rumble, and favored her with an approving smile.

Stevie's smile was uncharacteristically demure. "This is the investigator I told you about. Henry Spain."

Sturtevant had a powerful grip, and he made too much of it. He ushered us in and threw a wary glance outside before he closed the door. A shoulder gun stood on its butt plate next to the hinges. Sturtevant saw me looking at it.

"Ever see one of these, Spain?" He picked it up and broke it open. "Half rifle and half shotgun. .22 Magnum in the top barrel, 410 gauge in the bottom. I load with hollow point over buckshot."

"Any particular reason?"

He closed the weapon and put it back. "Like I told the L.A. cops, I wear boots. When I find tracks from expensive hiking shoes outside my trailer, it tells me I've had uninvited guests."

He cleared papers from a couch so his invited guests could sit down. To appearances he was a marginal soul hacking out something resembling a living in an isolated trailer full of books and strong coffee smell.

Stevie and I both declined his brew.

"When did you talk to the police?" I asked.

"They drove out the morning after Stephanie told them about our meeting."

He lumbered around behind a cluttered desk and settled into a chair that groaned under his weight.

"The man killed in East L.A. was shot by someone who mistook him for me."

"You don't look anything like the dead man."

"All I told Stephanie was to look for a cream colored station wagon in the parking lot across from a Mexican restaurant I knew about."

Stevie nodded agreement.

"Told her how?" They obviously hadn't met before.

He patted a laptop computer sitting open on the desk.

"Why didn't you keep the appointment?"

"On the way I noticed a persistent pair of headlights in the mirror. I lost whoever it was, but I also lost myself. I'm from Arizona. I don't navigate well in L.A. By the time I arrived the cops had the street blocked. I got a flashlight in my eyes and an order to move along."

I glanced at Stevie. "Were you on time?"

"I had a night flying lesson. My student was late."

It sounded like the killer might have been the only one who showed up on schedule. Working from only an intercepted e-mail, he popped the first likely prospect.

"Did you two also use E-mail to set up this morning's meeting?" I asked.

"Why?" Sturtevant glanced at Stevie.

"Someone tried to kill us on the way here." Her tone suggested the incident alone validated all her suspicions about her father's death.

Sturtevant scowled at me, as if I were personally responsible for putting her in harm's way. I gave him the play-by-play, with enough color commentary to let him know I didn't appreciate being dragged into his problems.

"Why don't you tell me what's going on?"

He looked me over like a master craftsman sizing up a none-too-promising apprentice, wondering whether to trust me with the secrets of the ages.

"What were you doing during the Vietnam War, Spain?"

"Fighting in it."

He cocked an eyebrow at me. "When I was a young journalist out to make my name and change the world, I went to Vietnam. I planned to expose the war in a series of hard hitting articles, maybe testify before Congress on what I'd seen, then move on to cure racism, poverty, pollution and a litany of other social ills."

He emitted a chuckle over his youthful innocence—a high-pitched, wheezy sound, like he had swallowed a tin whistle in the middle of an asthma attack. When it didn't earn him anything but an impatient look, he got serious.

"Like everyone else, I saw the PX goods in street vendors' stalls and the drugs as cheap as candy and the young b-girls being groomed for whorehouses. I raged inwardly at the venal businessmen and corrupt officials who would degrade a decent and placid society for their own gain, but I was sure in my heart that I was after bigger game. Time and fate proved me wrong."

Sturtevant fortified himself with a slug of coffee.

"Some years later I was a reporter in Phoenix, reduced from lofty ideals to grubbing for daily tidbits of truth. The Capo of a New York Mafia family moved there. One enterprising member of the fourth estate asked why and had his car blown up, with him in it. An army of investigative reporters smelled Pulitzer and moved in. They left empty handed."

"Is there a point to all this?" I asked. "Or did we just happen to show up during story hour?"

Sturtevant's look suggested he was tolerating me only for Stevie's benefit. "How much do you know about currency fluctuation in the third world, Spain?"

"What should I know?"

"Hyperinflation can destroy entire economies. Money can literally become worthless. To protect themselves, people hoard gold. When they need cash, they sell it on the black market. That's what the mob was doing in Phoenix. Laundering illicit gold through front companies dealing in precious metals. Bullion bought in Vietnam with the profits of prostitution and dope peddling; smuggled from Saigon by U.S. officials."

"Was Stevie's father involved?"

She bristled at the idea. "Harold Lomax tricked him."

Sturtevant gave her a reassuring grin. "Lomax had no reason to tell the air crew what they were flying."

"Harold Lomax has been dead for two weeks," I reminded them. "He didn't kill anyone in East L.A. on Friday."

"Harold Lomax's superior in Saigon, the man who put him up to this scheme, is still very much alive."

"Does he have a name?"

"Brigadier General Franklin Winter, retired."

"What did the police think of that idea?" I asked.

"If it was the mob that wanted me dead, I'd've been buried eight years ago when this was published."

Sturtevant picked up a hardbound book. The title, *Blood Money*, was splashed in crimson across the jungle green dust jacket. Representing the cast of characters were a sloe-eyed Asian doxie, a fat-faced oriental businessman, a ranking American military officer and a human refrigerator. The police had probably been as skeptical as I was.

"Is that still in print?"

"I have my publisher's assurance, in writing, that it will be reprinted in revised form and promoted aggressively if significant fresh evidence is developed. That is what General Franklin Winter is afraid of."

"Saigon fell a quarter of a century ago. The statute of limitations on smuggling has long since expired."

Stevie bolted to her feet and glared down at me. "Franklin Winter killed my father."

Sturtevant was more circumspect in his theories. "Numerous potential witnesses have died other than natural deaths since the scheme was closed out. If any of those deaths can be connected with the conspiracy, Winter can be charged with felony murder."

"Have you any actual evidence that the death of Stevie's father is related to your conspiracy?"

Sturtevant held the book across the desk. "Spain, I promise you when you have read this and learned what you and your friends really struggled and died for in Vietnam, you'll be fighting mad."

"I'll read it," I agreed, standing to collect the volume. "I'll also talk to General Winter."

Sturtevant gave me another wheezy laugh. "Do you really think you can do what I haven't been able to in eight years of trying?"

"I'm not from Arizona. I do know how to navigate in L.A."

My confidence brought a flicker of hope to Sturtevant's eyes. "You can find him in Holmby Hills. Not far from the Playboy Mansion, in fact. Ensconced in the tawdry splendor for which he bankrupted his soul."

Sturtevant showed us out, pumping my hand and telling me what a pleasure it had been to meet me. Stevie frowned at me when I tossed his book on the back seat of the Volvo.

"I thought you were going to read it." She waved good-bye to Sturtevant as I pulled away from his trailer. "Well, you are, aren't you?"

"Don't get your hopes up, Stevie. Sturtevant lives on a percentage of whatever his publisher can sell. The more sensation he can whip up, the better he does."

"His facts had to be checked by lawyers so the publishers wouldn't get sued, didn't they?"

I didn't have an answer for that. "Did you find Sturtevant, or did he find you?"

"My mom had a copy of his book. I read it a lot, and started wondering if he knew stuff he didn't put in. So I wrote him at the publisher and sent him my E-mail address."

"Did he sic you on Harold Lomax?"

"Nobody sicced me on anyone."

"What was your relationship with Lomax?"

"You're really a granny, aren't you?"

"Humor me."

"It was your basic parking meter romance. He wondered how much money he'd have to put into this chick before she came across and I wondered whether he'd expire before I got what I wanted."

Lame comedy was the last thing I needed. "You were driving his Bentley."

"He loaned it to me while he went to some charity dinner. It wasn't the kind of function where the old boys took their latest squeeze, so he told me to catch a movie and pick him up after. Only he got run over by some drunk. I didn't know what to do with the car, so I drove it until the repo creepos got it yesterday."

"Did Lomax give you any reason to believe Sturtevant's conspiracy theory?"

"It's real," she snapped. "At least read the book before you treat it like JFK and black helicopters." She tugged the hem of her skirt down to her knees and stared out the windshield.

The silent treatment gave me time to come to terms with Alex Sturtevant and his loopy tale. I didn't attach any importance to the persistent lights behind him the night he was supposed to meet Stevie. Interstate 10 was a straight run into Boyle Heights. He had probably been spooked by a dowager herding her designer SUV back from Palm Springs.

Eladio Aguilar was a different story. He was dead, possibly because he parked his light colored station wagon where someone expected Alex Sturtevant's light colored station wagon to be parked.

I dropped Stevie and went back to my office to curl up with *Blood Money.* It was easy to see why it hadn't sold. Sturtevant liked to preach. The whole thing read like a sermon against rapacious western incursion into genteel oriental culture. He had anecdotal evidence of corruption and photocopies of the ledgers of a Phoenix precious metals firm whose owner had been found murdered in the desert, but no link between the two until April, 1975.

According to Sturtevant, the story climaxed just before the fall of Saigon. Tons of gold remained in private hoards in the city. The North Vietnamese were closing in fast. Desperate profiteers turned to General Franklin Winter. Winter turned to police advisor Harold Lomax. Lomax arranged for an Air America freighter to haul the loot from Bien Hoa to a small airfield at the edge of the desert near Los Angeles. There it was picked up by unnamed contacts Lomax supposedly had in the CIA and trucked to Mob fronts in Phoenix; all in violation of U.S. law, the public trust and Alex Sturtevant's personal code of outrage.

Sturtevant called his version of the flight of the Starliner a reconstruction. To me it looked more like a wild guess. And I had an uneasy feeling he had guessed wrong on key pieces of the narrative.

The only man in a position to know the truth was Brigadier General Franklin Winter, retired. I was pretty sure I could con him into seeing me, but I didn't know how much I could persuade him to tell me.

CHAPTER 11

General Franklin Winter's estate and his secrets lay hidden behind a high brick wall. A discreet placard on a metal speaker box instructed me to press the button, announce my name clearly and wait. Wrought iron gates opened without a whisper. I knew the silent movement resulted from nothing more sinister than electricity and bearing grease, but the effect was still spooky.

An asphalt drive curved up through manicured oriental shrubbery to a huge house akin to nothing I had ever seen. The main section rose two stories, the upper terraced and narrowing to a glass brick chimney. From the lower, flat-roofed wings radiated like helicopter blades. Muted door chimes brought a man of fifty. His haircut was regulation Marine Corps, and he looked fit.

"I am Major Cole, aide to General Winter." A sport coat and open collar dress shirt translated that to retired major and personal assistant. "You have a letter of introduction for the General?"

I handed him a copy of the engagement letter that had come from Paige Lomax in the morning's mail. He didn't bother to read it. He let me in, told me to wait and disappeared down a hall.

The main section of the mansion was built on a scale that reduced a nine-foot Steinway to a corner piece; a single pristine room where matching furniture stood in precise formation, awaiting inspection. Sunlight infiltrated through the glass chimney and through more glass beneath the eaves of the terraces overhead. Winter's money had turned nature into his private chandelier.

Major Cole returned.

"The General will see you."

He led me down a hall and ushered me into a study. The walls were hung with the souvenirs of a command level military career, including citations for decorations so lofty I had only heard of them. The desk was carved teak; massive, polished and beyond price. Behind it sat a gaunt man in a bulky cardigan; a man to whom the advancing years had not been kind. His liver-splotched scalp showed through a thin cover of snow-white hair. A small blood vessel had burst at the corner of one eye and spread a spontaneous bruise over the cheekbone below. He peered at me intently, as if neither eye focused easily.

"You were a soldier, sir," he finally said in a voice that originated in his throat rather than his diaphragm, and sounded perilously close to cracking.

"Many years ago, General."

Paige Lomax's letter lay on the desk in front of Alex Sturtevant's arch villain, under a large magnifying lens adjusted so the old General could read it with minimum strain on his dwindling resources.

"This is a photocopy, sir."

The original was locked in my safe deposit box. "You are welcome to call Mrs. Lomax to authenticate it."

I had called before I left the office and learned Paige would be in deposition all morning. Winter had probably had Major Cole do the same and knew he would have to rely on the letter.

"This says you are to investigate the background of Cynthia Lomax. It was Harold Lomax whom I knew."

"But it was Cynthia who met the Starliner when it landed in California."

A pitying smile touched his bloodless lips. "You have read a book by one of life's pathetic spectators, and now you come to accuse me. Is that the purpose of your visit, Mr. Spain?"

"To ask you, General. I mean you no harm. I just want some information that may help people come to terms with their dead relatives."

The old man gathered his strength and stood. "Come walk with me, Mr. Spain."

Major Cole didn't like the idea, but he apparently knew better than to object or follow. General Winter walked slowly, holding himself erect with visible effort. I didn't think it was for my benefit. The emotional defeat of surrendering the bearing he had carried since West Point was probably worse in his mind than any physical discomfort.

"I presume," he said as we came into the grand hall of his mansion, "that you have at some time in your life been forced to terms with your own moral frailty. That you will not be shocked if I dispense with the traditional hypocrisies."

"I don't shock easily, General."

"I found my own moral bottom in mountains of Northern Korea. Are you familiar with the history of the War?"

"No, sir." Military history had never interested me. Not even the little bit I participated in.

"In the last desperate weeks of 1950, UN Forces were being driven relentlessly southward by Chinese field armies many times our size. Casualties were appalling. Officers doubled as riflemen to hold beleaguered positions. That December was the coldest in living memory. We fought over ground frozen too hard to dig foxholes. We had little food, and no proper clothing. The Chinese had even less, as I learned to my everlasting horror on Christmas night.

"A parachute flare went off overhead, and by its light I saw a human wave of advancing Chinese soldiers. One was making directly for my position. The great fear that lurks in every infantryman's heart is that he will one day become the focus of a single enemy bent only upon killing him. That the impersonal carnage of war will become intensely and fatally personal."

I didn't say anything. I didn't have to. He knew from a glance at my eyes that I recalled the feeling as if Vietnam had happened yesterday.

"When I saw that Chinese soldier coming at me out of the night and the blowing snow, I was seized by a terror beyond all description or reason. I fired my carbine empty trying to stop him. I could see bullets rip into the fabric of his uniform as he closed on me. Panic robbed me of coordination. I could not reload. Weak from hunger and fatigue, with only a bayonet to defend myself, I was certain my end had come. But fate had worse in store for me.

"The man fell dead not a foot from where I lay and I saw the awful truth. He was not armed. He had lost his weapon, along with whatever will he might once have possessed. Frozen and spent, he had walked like a zombie with his assaulting comrades, coming at me only by the blind chance of war, too far gone even to feel the bullets I fired through him. He died of massive hemorrhage, I suppose. A helpless soul wandering he knew not where, murdered by an American officer who as a youth had sat in movie theaters outraged at images of Allied air crews machine-gunned in their parachutes by Axis fighter pilots."

It was a long speech for weary lungs. The old General tottered along in silence for a minute, catching his breath.

"Being the son of a flag officer, and surviving what the armed forces wished to portray as a successful rear guard action, I received the nation's second highest award for valor. Official recognition of my performance was my father's highest validation of his faith in me. The private truth of the matter was for me the ultimate notice of my own moral inadequacy."

We had crossed the grand hall to another wing of the house. General Winter opened a door into a cavernous garage where automobiles stood with the sheen and symmetry of a museum exhibit.

"The motor cars I admired as a young man," Winter explained. "Luxuries I could not then afford and can now enjoy only vicariously. Built with uncompromising excellence by men with the courage and vision to ignore the nattering pygmies who would have squandered the cost of design and construction to feed the starving masses."

The Ferrari Europa was probably worth somewhere north of a million dollars. Others had names like Delahaye and Talbot Lago and values I couldn't begin to estimate. I put my hands in my pockets so I wouldn't be tempted to leave any finger smudges as we wandered along.

"It's an impressive collection," I said, "but why bother showing it to me?"

"You are here to ask about the illicit movement of investment quality gold from Southeast Asia to the United States during the Vietnam War, are you not?"

"Yes, sir."

"Some of the story I cannot tell you because it pre-dated my posting to Saigon. If you wish to hear the rest, you must suffer my motives along with the facts."

"I would have asked about them anyway."

The old man nodded satisfaction. "When I arrived in January, 1975, the military situation had already deteriorated beyond recovery. The pathetic charade of smuggling gold in diplomatic pouches could not hope to move the hoard that remained in private hands in the capitol. The choice in my mind was to leave this fortune for a backward government to squander in a hopeless effort to crush the human spirit into the mindless mold of agrarian communism, or evacuate it to the United States where it would be placed in banks that would loan it to men of vision who would use it to build an expanding future.

"I took it upon myself, without leave from my superiors or consultation with my peers, to move the gold, in the full knowledge that its provenance was as foul as any treasure accumulated by man, to where I thought it might do some good for mankind. I take no credit for the downfall of communism, sir, but I do take a deep and abiding pride in the small part only a man already shorn of his moral illusions could have played in holding it at bay until it destroyed itself."

"An old soldier," I quoted not unkindly from the farewell address of Douglas MacArthur, "who tried to do his duty as God gave him the light to see that duty?"

"To spare you the temptation of further snide comment, sir, it is also true that I was admirably positioned to extort a share of the bounty for myself."

"Which you shared with Cynthia Lomax in return for handling the actual transport."

"With Harold Lomax," he corrected.

"I know about New Year's Eve, 1944, General."

Winter's smile told me he had agreed to see me at least in part to learn what I knew, and had walked me away from Major Cole to ensure that no embarrassments were broadcast.

"In 1944, you understand, there was no atomic bomb. No quick way to end the war with Japan. Invasion of the home islands was certain, as was my participation. The life expectancy of an infantry lieutenant in close combat was, at that time, variously reckoned between seventeen and thirty seconds. The more I drank that New Year's Eve, the clearer things became to me. Fate was offering me dalliance with a blonde goddess as consolation for the ultimate sacrifice soon to be demanded."

"A goddess who later tracked you down."

"In spite of the fact that I wore no nameplate," Winter marveled, "and never mind that the gales of war carried me within days to the farthest corner of the earth."

"You're still alive, so you must have made your peace with her."

He stopped at a slope-backed coupe, resplendent in chocolate and beige.

"Do you recognize the marque, sir?"

"A Bentley Continental R."

"Cynthia asked a few years before she died that I buy it from a storage facility and preserve rather than restore it that she might visit it on occasion."

"When did she find you?"

"She contacted me in 1956, by which time she had also found and forsaken love. The man once owned this Bentley. He was, for reasons I never came to know, unable to give her either marriage or children, both of which she then desired. We agreed that if I could make satisfactory arrangements to secure her future, my wartime indiscretion would become a permanent part of the past."

"You fixed her up with Harold Lomax."

"Son of a socially prominent California family that barely weathered the depression; an attorney reduced to a career in law enforcement; an introvert who, in spite of considerable social grace, would never on his own pursue a woman to the point of marriage. Cynthia was forceful and still stunningly beautiful. She also had money, the source of which I never learned."

Sigrid Helstrom had reached into the darkest corner of her past to make the jump to respectable society as Cynthia Lomax. Twenty years later, when her chance at real wealth came, she reverted long enough to meet a Starliner carrying tons of contraband gold. And through it all she couldn't forget Malcolm Trevor, the man who never laid a hand on her. There was a hell of a love story in there somewhere, but it was probably wasted on men like Winter and me.

"I would like to know," I said as we walked out of the garage, "why you told me as much as you did."

"Should you try to publicize what you have learned this morning, you will find, as Mr. Sturtevant found before you, that no one is interested. Those whom you wish to inform will simply yawn in your face."

"You don't get many visitors, do you, General?"

"Those of my generation who have not already died, sir, have grown too feeble to travel easily, if at all. My children and grand-children have found their own lives, and I have no wish to burden them."

"I amused you. I was someone you could play with, like a cat with a ball of yarn."

"You put yourself into my hands, sir. You were entitled to no quarter."

"Nor will you be, General, when the spotlight focuses on you."

"Mr. Spain, when opportunity came, I seized it. When power was mine, I abused it. Today I live with frivolous extravagance while much of the world goes hungry and illiterate. For such behavior a man may be envied, but never will he be reviled."

"Paige Lomax is going to campaign for a seat on the City Council. Her opponents will make an issue of the source of her wealth. And by extension, yours."

I left the old General scowling and drove to my office troubled by what I had learned. Sigrid Helstrom had killed three men only peripherally connected with her violation, but hadn't bothered even to contact one of the principals until a dozen years later. That meant there was something going on that I didn't understand. Ramona Benitez had claimed to know everything about Sigrid. Maybe she knew the answer. I picked up the phone and learned otherwise.

Marisol was first up on voice mail. Ramona had slipped away in her sleep. The service was at St. Gregory's. I was expected. I spent the drive out to Telegraph Avenue and Victoria wondering what, if anything, Ramona had left behind. And trying not to wonder if my visit had shortened what little time she had left.

CHAPTER 12

"Senor Espain?"

I looked up from the guest book to see a sad-faced woman in a black mantilla reading my signature upside down. She waved a plump hand. A muscular young usher made his way across the anteroom, parting the crowd of arriving mourners like a Navy cruiser coming through heavy seas. If it were trouble, I wouldn't need an ambulance. The kid was big enough to throw me to the nearest hospital.

He nodded obediently at some rapid Spanish from the woman. I wasn't sure I'd understood correctly until the kid escorted me into the cathedral and installed me in the second pew from the front. I was a favored guest at the funeral of a woman I'd spoken to only once and left in tears.

The few other anglo faces I could see without being obvious were closer to Ramona's age than mine; probably her last surviving friends from Hollywood. The service was rendered in a mix of Spanish and English, an eloquent eulogy for a woman trying to find her way in the twilight between two cultures. By the time it ended I had spotted Marisol partway down in the pew ahead of mine. I timed my exit to catch her.

"Mi sentido pesame," I said in a shameless attempt to curry favor. It was Marisol who sat at Ramona's knee and listened to the tales of a bygone Hollywood. If I wanted Ramona's secrets, I would have to finagle them from her.

"Thank you for coming, Mr. Spain. It was my grand mother's last wish."

It clearly wasn't Marisol's. She turned to help an elderly gentleman up to the bier. I took his other arm to make myself useful.

Ramona looked even tinier than I remembered. Without life in her dark eyes she was a waxen doll set out in the full feminine regalia of her ancestral Mexican homeland. Maybe it was just the organ music, but I had a creepy feeling that even in death she wasn't done with me.

Marisol was. An usher took the old gentleman and she moved off to be with family. That was my cue to join the departing mourners. A familiar voice ambushed me.

"You son of a bitch," Roy Lee Exum said in her quiet Cape Cod drawl.

I hadn't expected to run across an associate professor of cinema at the funeral of a long-forgotten B-movie player. Not that I objected. Roy Lee's kind of sophisticated appeal only got better in basic black. The venom in her eyes just made her more intriguing.

"Hello," was all I could think of to say.

"Don't 'hello' me. You had a seat next to Alan Devon."

"You mean the old guy?"

"I mean the director with sixty one films to his credit. Never has he sat for more than cursory interviews, let alone had his biography written."

"Publish or perish?"

"Damn you, Spain. I was the one who gave you the lead to Ramona. You could have called and mentioned you had been invited and would I like to decorate your arm."

"I'm sorry," I said as the crowd carried us out the main doors. "I had an hour's notice and no idea what kind of reception I'd get."

She gave me the silent treatment.

"I also had no way to know you trolled Hollywood funerals for leads," I reminded her. "Can I walk you to your car?"

"I came with some other faculty. You can drive me back." She put enough ice in her voice to keep me from getting any wrong ideas. "And on the way you can tell me what you've learned."

The fact that Roy Lee wanted to know what I had learned meant she had good reason to believe there was something to learn. The fact that she was prepared to let me take her back to UCLA to find out what it was said more. Normally she wouldn't get caught in the same zip code with me.

"Work car," I explained when she wrinkled her nose at the Volvo.

"You ought to retire it. It looks old enough."

"Someone tried yesterday."

"Was that meant to sound ominous?"

"Just don't assign any graduate students to Sigrid Helstrom. At least not for a while."

I held the door for her to get in. She had the kind of grace that was worth staring at even in a long skirt. I didn't know how she had come by it. I didn't know anything about her, except that she was a single mother raising two boys on an associate professor's salary and whatever consulting and writing she could manage to do. Apparently her prince had come and gone, leaving her in a world of frogs. I closed her in with solicitude befitting my station, went around and got behind the wheel.

She sniffed delicately. "Shalimar, Mr. Spain, is one of those fragrances best used in extreme moderation."

"I wear it so seldom I get carried away." I cranked the engine to life. "What did you turn up on Sigrid Helstrom?"

"You first."

Backing out of the parking slot and getting us into traffic on Victoria gave me time to get my brain in gear. I wasn't about to risk Paige Lomax's wrath for a few academic tidbits, but it occurred to me Roy Lee would be interested only in film lore, and the gossip that went with it.

"She was Malcolm Trevor's cutie."

"Trevor," she said with a convincing level of surprise. "*Confidential* magazine was after him for years."

Confidential had been the first of the glossy Hollywood scandal rags. "What did they find?"

"Nobody knows. Word was that they finally got the goods on him late in fifty-six. It took more than a year to double-check and document their story. Just before the article was scheduled to go to press, they lost a criminal libel suit and folded. Their file on Trevor vanished."

Nineteen fifty-six was the year Sigrid Helstrom checked out of the film industry to marry Harold Lomax. "Who exactly was Trevor?"

"Film doctor."

"What's a film doctor?"

"Movies," she said in a patient voice she probably used with slow students, "are made in a hermetically sealed environment. They are written, directed, acted and edited by people who have very little contact with the real world. No one knows how the public will react to them. Trevor would go to the initial release and dissect audience reaction. Based on his observations, poorly received films would be re-cut. If something got the audience's adrenaline pumping, or its tears flowing, they'd splice in more—they usually had three feet of film they didn't use for every foot they did—and the parts that flopped wound up on the cutting room floor."

"His name would have been buried pretty far down in the credits, wouldn't it?"

"No credit for Mr. Trevor. Even today the executives who risk their massive egos making the initial decisions on films don't like to admit there is a post-release process."

"Then why would the scandal mongers have been interested in him? Even if the guy was an axe murderer, he wouldn't have been news unless Hollywood had already made him a household word."

"That's an excellent question," she said, sounding surprised that I had it in me. "Is there anything in Sigrid Helstrom's background that would shed any light?"

I shook my head. Not that Sigrid hadn't been up to her blonde tresses in dirty doings. But as far as I knew, no one involved had the name recognition it would take to sell her hijinks at the supermarket check out stand.

"How did you happen to know about Trevor?" I asked.

"His name has come up in interviews I've done. He seemed to have more money and power than his position could have provided. No one I talked to could tell me how he had come by it. It's always intrigued me. Like one of those Chinese puzzle cubes that sits on your desk for years because you can't figure it out."

"What about Helstrom?"

"What about her?"

"You wouldn't be riding in a Mesozoic Volvo with a Neanderthal like me if you hadn't learned something that did more than just pique your interest."

Roy Lee had a low-pitched laugh that sent electricity up my spine. "And here I thought I was being so clever."

"What did you learn?"

"After we talked, I started wondering why Helstrom had never been interviewed. At least for recollections of her work with bigger names. It occurred to me an interview might have been done, but not put on the computer yet, so I went back to the manual records. Sure enough, an interview was assigned."

"Can I get a copy?"

"Assigned but never done."

"Why not?"

"The grad student, who is now a first reader at Paramount, told me the assignment was canceled."

"Why?"

"No reason," she said. "Just canceled."

"Did somebody lean on the Dean?"

"Leave the poetry to Longfellow. And yes, obviously. The department depends on film industry cooperation for every facet of its operations."

"So anyone with a little pull could have shut down a routine biographical assignment on a tenth rate actress."

"But why would they want to? And why would the same thing happen with Ramona Benitez?"

I had some ideas on the subject, but I didn't want Roy Lee poking around in anything remotely dangerous. "I do know someone took a shot at me yesterday morning. If you're planning to ask questions, you might want to ask carefully."

She gave me a dubious look. "Helstrom and Trevor have been dead for years."

"It happened," I insisted.

"Are you sure it wasn't just your personality? You do rub some people the wrong way."

I wasn't sure of anything. I had blundered into a murder in East L.A. and followed a trail that led me to a long-dead B-movie actress. Stevie and I had been shot at following another trail that led back to the same actress. Sigrid seemed to be the common denominator. But of what I didn't know. All I really had was a prickly feeling that opening her background had put me in someone's gun sights.

"It was an ambush," I said, "and it wasn't set in one of my usual haunts."

"Speaking of haunts, mine is just ahead. And so far you haven't told me what you got from Ramona Benitez."

"Strictly speaking, you didn't give me Ramona's name. I paid for it."

"See why people shoot at you?"

"But I will trade you."

"What for what, the poor woman asked, knowing she was about to be victimized again."

"Ramona wanted Malcolm Trevor for herself," I said. "Can you check for anything that might link them?"

"Anything in particular?" Suspicion was a black border around the question.

"Anything that might tell where they were on New Year's Eve, 1944."

"That's pretty specific." Her Cape Cod drawl became an accusation. "You know something."

"Something happened at a nightclub called The Shadows. I thought I had a good fix on it, but the more I learn, the less I seem to know."

"What was it?"

"That's my end of the trade."

"All right," she agreed, too easily. "I'll see what I can find out." She either knew something already, or knew where she could find it.

I let her off at the edge of the campus. Watching her walk away I wondered if she intrigued me on her own considerable merits or if she just represented a world I had never gotten closer to than the university extension courses I had squeezed into a past life. Not that it mattered. She was out of my league and too smart to have anything to do with me. I headed back to my office with the windows open to evacuate the remains of Stevie's Shalimar.

On the way I thought about Malcolm Trevor, the autoerotic voyeur whom *Confidential* magazine had chased for reasons I couldn't begin to guess. He had known about Sigrid Helstrom's take down robbery of the Caliente Beach Club and kept it quiet, but probably not for money. He was already driving a Bentley before it happened. On the salary of a man who fixed bad movies and never got his name on the credits. But who, if I was inferring correctly from what Ramona had told me, had enough pull to sponsor film careers for both her and Sigrid.

I quit thinking about him when I got downtown and picked up the phone to check my voice mail. Paige Lomax wanted me in her office as soon as I could get there. She didn't sound happy.

CHAPTER 13

Paige Lomax roosted with the vultures in Century City, on the bones of the old Fox Studio, where once young women not unlike Sigrid and Ramona had come starry-eyed and learned the price of playing small roles in the celluloid fantasy that gave the nation refuge from its demons and its drudgery. Bodies and souls were still bartered in the hollow towers of steel and glass, but now the prizes were titles, bonuses and lofty offices with views all the way to the Pacific Ocean. The understudies and the bit players sorted mail, counted beans and sat behind big reception counters to tell visitors like me they would have to wait. Important people always needed to see you right away, and they were always busy when you got there.

At least Berkut and Shroeder's chairs were comfortable. I was absorbed in an article about drug smugglers stealing private airplanes when a shadow fell over the *Wall Street Journal* I had appropriated from the side table.

"Mr. Spain. I am sorry to have kept you waiting."

The earnest apology from Paige Lomax only reminded me that we were meeting on her turf and her terms.

"Would you come this way, please?"

She led me along a hallway hung with modern art. Her window office wasn't prime real estate, but it was enough to suggest she was a comer. I helped myself to a chair. She established herself behind a desk with her back to a matching credenza that held a monitor and keyboard.

"General Winter called me. He was not happy, and rightfully so."

"Not happy about my visit? Or not happy because your ambitions could expose his past to investigation?"

Her indignant glare put me on notice that I was here to be dressed down, not to ask impertinent questions. "Mr. Spain, General Winter is a former associate of the late Harold Lomax. You were retained under privilege to review the background of Cynthia Lomax. You misused my letter of engagement to impose on the General."

"Mrs. Lomax, you hired me to learn what your adversaries might learn before they learned it. I can't do that unless I think and act as they will think and act."

"General Winter would not have spoken to you without a letter from me. Certainly not about the Sturtevant libels."

"Winter was a soldier, highly decorated in the war against communism. To him, and to the men whose respect he would value, crimes committed to keep a hoard of gold out of communist hands were acts of valor. Risks taken above and beyond the call of duty. Sturtevant's version is just the way Winter wants the story told."

Paige limited her displeasure to a poker faced stare, which told me I'd hit on something she didn't want to talk about.

"You see, Mrs. Lomax, the thing that bothers me about Sturtevant's version is why the Starliner landed in California when the gold was bound for Phoenix. Why transfer it to slow moving ground transportation and risk inspection, break-down, hijacking and God knows what else?"

"And what did the General have to say about that?"

"I think the Starliner landed in California because Cynthia was in California. She wanted to deduct the Lomax family share before the loot went on to people in Phoenix who might forget to pay up."

"I asked what the General said. Not what you thought."

"Cynthia Lomax gave the orders. She had enough on the man to ruin him."

"Nonsense."

"Enough to blackmail him into arranging her marriage to Harold Lomax."

The idea elicited a metallic sound that was almost a laugh. I replied with a malicious grin.

"You don't seriously think a Stanford educated lawyer would pick a thirty-something veteran of who knows how many casting couches on his own, do you?"

Paige stiffened and her chair bumped gently against the credenza, just enough to clear the screen saver from the monitor. What came up was a cute picture of an open jail. The name in the input box was Victor Bradley. Probably her high profile pro-bono parole case. She caught me looking and cleared the screen.

"How much of the Sturtevant book would survive independent investigation?"

I tried not to fidget. "Well, that's the problem. Sturtevant's claims of fact had to be proven to his publisher's attorneys, so we can be pretty sure of those. But his reconstruction based on those facts doesn't make sense. So we're dealing with missing facts, faulty reasoning or some combination of the two. An independent investigation could find new facts, draw other conclusions from the existing ones or both. It's just not predictable."

"How long before you will know?"

"Two days, I think, to run down the leads I have now. The outcome will depend on what I find."

"You are not to contact General Winter again without my express permission."

I held up my hands up in a silent gesture of surrender. Winter wasn't likely to talk to me again anyway.

"I shall expect your report in two days" she said. "At that time I'll decide whether to continue your engagement."

Paige's Dragon Lady routine had turned into used Kleenex. I had to remind myself that her lawyer-client privilege was all the protection I had until I got to the bottom of this. It couldn't happen too soon.

"Is there anything you can tell me that might speed the process along?"

"No. There isn't. Now, if you will excuse me, Mr. Spain, I have a probation hearing to prepare for."

"Does the pro bono work mean you've already made a firm decision to run for the council?"

"For your information, Victor Bradley is a brilliant young man. His IQ has been tested at one hundred fifty six. He was convicted on the flimsiest of evidence, but he did not become bitter. He earned his computer science degree in prison—no small feat. Parole will allow him to contribute to society, rather than burdening it."

"That's a nice speech, Mrs. Lomax, but it doesn't answer the question."

"I don't think it's any of your business."

"Maybe not, but I would like to know why I'm being followed."

"Followed?" Her surprise seemed genuine.

"A gray BMW picked me up outside your house the other night."

"Not on my instructions."

She sounded worried enough to be telling the truth, which backed up my initial impression that the driver had been well below the talent she could afford.

"Did you tell anyone you'd hired me?"

"Certainly not. This is a highly sensitive matter."

I accepted the statement with a nod and stood up.

"I hope," she said, "that you haven't been careless in your questioning and drawn attention to yourself."

"I promise you, Mrs. Lomax, I will find out who it is." I wasn't supposed to be the one on the wrong end of surveillance.

She lifted her desk phone. "Please send Mr. Bradley back in."

Victor Bradley was in his late twenties. A weight-room build kept his suit coat from draping properly. Variations in skin tone suggested his short haircut and clean shave were recent. He gave me a friendly smile and stood aside to let me pass. I took it for a prison yard con job. Whatever he had done to get shut up must have been pretty serious if he had done enough time to earn a college degree and was still looking for probation. I made bail for the Volvo at the garage kiosk and pulled onto the street.

A glance in the mirror told me the BMW was back. When I told Paige Lomax I would find out who was following me, I had visions of reading DMV information off my computer screen. But DMV hadn't found Stevie for me, and they might strike out again.

"Carpe diem," I told myself, then couldn't remember if that meant seize the moment or beware of the moment.

I drove until I found a self-serve gas station located on a busy corner with an arterial stoplight controlling the intersection.

The BMW pulled to the curb in a transit zone. A glance told me the driver was a scrawny stranger; denim jacket, straggly hair, facial scruff. His sallow complexion suggested a recent encounter with the corrections system, but otherwise he was generic urban trash. He ate from a fast food bag perched on the dashboard and seemed content to watch me pump gas. Replacing the hose, I stowed my credit card receipt and started the Volvo.

The intersection light turned red. Traffic backed up quickly and froze the BMW against the curb. Pulling ahead through the pump island, I made a right turn and joined the traffic flow on the cross street. A strip mall blocked the BMW from my view, and my Volvo from his. I pulled into the parking lot and ducked into an empty stall. A minute later the BMW rolled past out on the street. I rejoined the traffic flow a block behind.

It was that easy. The guy was a complete amateur. He switched lanes, frantically scanning the traffic ahead to locate me. After a few blocks he gave it up and went on about whatever business he had. I followed him through downtown then south on Alameda, past Union Station and Little Tokyo, into the industrial section.

Grumbling semis became more plentiful and short strings of freight cars waited on rails embedded in the paving. The BMW turned onto a side street and found its way into a dirt lot behind a tavern. I drifted to the margin of the road and hid behind a filthy van.

A rickety fence separated the tavern lot from the street. Graffiti artists had turned it into a mural. The BMW was visible through a gap where someone had kicked a board out of the colorful fantasy. The driver was in no hurry to get out. He stuck a ragged cigarette in his mouth. It didn't seem to be a particularly good brand of hemp. He had to re-light it twice, and suck hard for whatever enjoyment he got. He was still jittery when he came out of the lot on foot. I gave him a block's head start.

This wasn't a suit and tie neighborhood. The air held a quiet that was sullen rather than peaceful, as if the close-packed little houses we passed knew their paint and landscaping money had gone for cheap liquor, and they resented it. My quarry walked with his eyes on the ground and his hands thrust into the pockets of worn jeans. His marijuana jag was winding down, and he kicked at stray cans and bits of trash with scuffed work boots. He stopped in front of an old brick apartment building, palmed something out of his jacket pocket, lifted a pant leg and slipped whatever it was into his sock. Then he disappeared inside.

According to a weathered sign over the entrance, I had found my way to Camelot. The door was set back in a dim enclosure. A shadow showed where mailboxes once had been fastened. A magnetic card reader secured the door. There was a mechanical back up, but my lock picks were safely hidden under a tray of wrenches in a toolbox in the trunk of the Volvo. I hoofed it back to the car.

While I was fishing out the slim jim to see what I could find in the BMW, two pair of chromed Harley Davidsons rumbled past on the street, ridden by rolling advertisements for steroid abuse. They pulled into the lot behind the tavern and shut down. I glanced through the gap in the fence.

One of the steroids draped himself over the trunk lid of the BMW like it was an easy chair.

"Where is the little shit?"

"Fuck him. I need a brew."

"Fuck you. We're working."

"Hey, I can handle it, man."

"I said we're working."

This wasn't the local honor society settling in for a pleasant hour of Parcheesi and literary criticism. I had stumbled onto something. A little voice in my head told me I was too old for this sort of thing, but the adrenaline rush drowned it out. I closed the trunk of the Volvo very quietly and got behind the wheel.

Ragged exhaust noise caught my ear. A dirty green GMC pick-up rolled past. It looked like the truck that ambushed Stevie and me. The two men inside were roughly dressed huskies; Slavic-featured strangers. They passed the Volvo without a glance. That bothered me. If they were the shooters, they should have recognized the car. They slowed and turned into the tavern lot. I rolled down my window to catch any conversation, but the men in the truck didn't seem in the mood to socialize with the motorcycle enthusiasts.

The man I had followed in the BMW was on his way back, engrossed in an animated conversation with a cell phone. He hustled into the lot, waving one arm like a platoon leader trying to summon a meeting of battle hardened squad sergeants. A minute later engines rumbled to life and the vehicles left in convoy. The BMW led the way, then the truck, followed by the Harleys in pairs. I brought up the rear a block back, eagerly reading license numbers into my recorder.

These jokers were going to rue the day they tangled with ace investigator Henry Spain. Of course, I wasn't sure why they would rue it. I hadn't got a license number when Stevie and I were ambushed, so I couldn't prove this GMC was that GMC. The guy in the BMW had as much right to follow me as I had to follow him. And the steroids had done nothing worse than look big and mean enough to pound the stuffing out of me if they realized I was behind them.

All I could do was tag along and hope that whatever felonies they were on their way to commit wouldn't be a burden on my medical insurance.

Chapter 14

My enthusiasm for surveillance waned as we rolled south in the gathering dusk. The convoy kept to side streets, leading me through neighborhoods where convenience stores looked like prisons and the basic food groups were Colt 45 and Night Train. We turned onto an industrial boulevard. Two of the Harleys peeled off and rumbled away down a side street. The GMC and the other two Harleys did the same a block later. The BMW eased to the margin of the road. I parked where I could watch through the glass of intervening cars.

A steady stream of moving headlights in the distance told me we were near the I-5, but otherwise I was lost. Passing traffic clicked off the minutes. My stomach reminded me how long it had been since lunch. My bladder chimed in with its own complaint. I flipped on the recorder and started dictating a summary of the afternoon's events.

I didn't know what to make of them. First a scruffy male Caucasian, name and affiliation unknown, had, not for the first time, tried to follow me in a disreputable BMW. I got behind him and he led me to a South Central apartment building with the unlikely name of Camelot. He was inside no more than ten minutes before he charged out, apparently at the behest of someone on the other end of a cell phone, to rendezvous with a group of obvious perpetrator types. I tagged along on what looked to be a mission of mischief and wound up parked on a rundown street with no more clue than I had when I started what it was all about. Motorcycle engines growled to life and I shut off the recorder.

The BMW's lights came on. The driver pulled out into traffic and made a fast right at the intersection, ignoring angry horns to talk into his cell phone. I started my engine to go after him. This time traffic had me pinned. When I was finally able to pull out into the flow the BMW was gone. The intersection light turned red and ended any hope of catching up. I sat there listening to the cycle engines rev.

The racket came from a yard with no address, just a hurricane fence strung through with privacy slats and topped by razor wire. A gate swung open. Two Harleys idled out. They weren't part of the group I'd seen earlier. The riders were lean, ropy Latinos in leather jackets and colorful head bandanas. An eighteen wheeler followed them out and made it through the intersection as the light changed. I wondered if this had something to do with the BMW's sudden departure. In a flash of stupidity I told myself it couldn't hurt to add to my collection of license numbers. I turned the corner and fell in behind the truck.

It was tagged for commerce in California and Mexico, so naturally I started wondering why and quit paying attention to my surroundings. A rumble of scavenger pipes prompted me to check the mirror. A '65 Impala low rider was on my bumper. From what the streetlights showed of the heavyweights inside, I didn't think they were cruising for chicks.

I had unwittingly inserted myself into the middle of another convoy. The two Harleys were riding scout. The Impala was the chase car, positioned to block any trouble from behind. A truck moving at night under that kind of security had to be carrying something both valuable and illegal. The men involved would be heavily armed and probably coked to the edges. Any sudden move would just draw attention to me.

The semi started up a ramp to the I-5. The smart move seemed to be to follow along like a square nuts Anglo bystander, slip into another lane once we were on the Interstate and disappear down the first off-ramp. If I didn't dissolve into a puddle of sweat first.

I hadn't forgotten the gang I followed to get here, but I had definitely underestimated their nerve. The GMC pickup appeared from nowhere and roared past me up the inside curve of the ramp. It turned sharply in front of the semi, cutting the rig off from the leading Harleys. The semi driver hit his brakes and I hit mine. Two steroids popped up in the bed of the GMC brandishing AK-47s. One of them opened up on the Harleys, sending the riders racketing up the ramp hunched over their handlebars. The other put a warning burst over the cab of the tractor.

"Get outta the fucking truck!"

I don't know if anyone complied. In the mirror I caught a flash of the Impala pulling out to get around me. The noise of two more Harleys jerked my head around. The two remaining steroids slid to a stop behind the Impala. They had heavy sub-machine guns; an M-3 grease gun and a Thompson with no shoulder stock. They raked the Impala with .45 hardball. Four Latinos bailed out as tires flattened and glass flew in a brilliant cascade of tiny shards. I didn't waste time shutting off the Volvo. I just rolled out and kissed the pavement.

Flat on my face in the street wasn't the best vantage point to sort out the confusion, but I did have a vague overall picture. It was a hijacking, of course. And someone had put considerable tactical thinking into it. The gang had stopped the semi on the ramp, cut it off from the scout element and ambushed the chase car. Now all they had to do was get someone into the tractor and motor off down the Interstate. The two steroids on Harleys could seal off the escape route as soon as they reloaded. I glanced under the semi.

A pair of legs was running from the GMC toward the tractor. Two quick shots came from the direction of the Impala. The legs stopped running. One of the Slavic huskies flopped face down in the street and didn't move. A Latino sprinted past me firing a heavy assault rifle. He almost stepped on me. His gunshots reverberated in my teeth. As soon as he was gone I started looking around frantically for a way out.

Horns were honking back on the arterial we had just left. Traffic had stopped and vehicles were backing up. Street lights showed peering faces behind automotive glass. Generations had been raised on the southern California fantasy that you'd always be safe as long as you didn't get out of the car.

Barely muffled motorcycle exhaust alerted me that one of the Latinos had found his way down from the Interstate and was hauling ass down the margin of the arterial, straight at the two steroids on Harleys. The guy had seen too many movies. He thought he could drive his cycle and shoot across the handlebars at the same time. Unfortunately the Ingram in his hand was real. He was spraying nine-millimeter all over the landscape. Ricochets would follow the surface of the street. I needed some cover. I made a fast crawl under the semi trailer.

The Latinos chose that moment to get the truck moving again. The trailer overhead magnified the racket of the Diesel engine. Huge tires began to turn inches from my head. There was a flurry of automatic gunfire as the tractor's bumper made contact with the GMC and shoved it aside. The semi's departure left me lying exposed in the street with no one for company but the fallen East European. I saw a pistol in his hand and scrambled that way fast.

Nobody shot me. For a moment it looked like my luck might hold. The battered GMC was limping off in pursuit of the semi. I could hear the two steroids on Harleys grumbling away down a side street to get ahead of the cargo. Two surviving Latinos from the disabled low rider were carjacking a Honda to go after the men trying to hijack their truck. The Latino on the cycle was reloading his Ingram to do the same. I was lying directly in his path.

The Slavic husky's pistol was a Soviet issue Makarov. I had never shot one before, but it looked like the time had come. I discovered I was shaking too badly to get a bead on the Latino, so I used the fallen man for an arm rest.

The Latino bore down on me with his Ingram spitting and popping. The Makarov worked flawlessly. My sight alignment was perfect. I saw the flash and the function of the slide. I saw the puff of dirt on his leather jacket. Nothing happened. Logic tried to tell me the pistol didn't have enough velocity to punch through whatever armor he was wearing under the jacket, but panic drowned it out. I couldn't think of anything but General Winter and the Chinese soldier advancing out of the Korean snow. I emptied the Makarov without ever changing my point of aim.

The Latino didn't hit me at all. He went past in a cloud of dust and hot exhaust and roared off in pursuit of the hijackers.

Suddenly I was alone.

Never one to waste an opportunity, I made it to the Volvo as fast as my rubber legs would carry me and squealed away in a shameless display of cowardice.

I don't remember how I got myself headed north on the I-5. I was trembling too badly to be driving at all, let alone on a jam-packed freeway. Thoughts started finding their way into my head. I had really done it to myself this time. I didn't know how many witnesses there had been to the hijack attempt. Probably dozens. I had visions of my license number on every police band in three counties. Armed and dangerous. Approach with caution. I knew my jitters were the aftermath of an adrenaline rush, but that didn't stop me watching the mirrors for blue strobes.

When I got home I was still too wired to eat. Liquor didn't help. I didn't dare go to bed. I was afraid I'd wake up with SWAT teams surrounding the house, yelling into a bullhorn for me to come out with my hands up. I turned on the TV.

I had missed the evening news. I sat mesmerized by a documentary on the Great Siberian Explosion. In 1908, blind chance had brought a massive chunk of space debris streaking into the Earth's atmosphere at twelve miles a second, where it created a fifteen megaton air burst that flattened hundreds of square miles of forest and lit the night sky for thousands of miles around.

I was as confused as the natives probably had been back then. I had no idea what had hit me. I felt like I remembered feeling after a firefight in Vietnam. I probably had the same thousand-yard stare.

CHAPTER 15

I woke up in the living room chair, shivering from the morning chill. The TV was still on. I flipped to the early news. Video showed the scene of last night's hijack attempt, with a hangover of yellow tape and blue strobes. A reporter chattered importantly. Two unidentified men were dead. No suspects were in custody. Anyone with information was urged to call police at the number on the screen. I shut it off.

A hot shower loosened the kinks of a cramped night and breakfast gave me some time to think through my predicament. If the police found a witness who remembered my license number, or if they lifted a traceable print from the Makarov I discarded when I panicked and ran, I was toast. Ditto if I turned myself in. They would prosecute me for assault with a deadly weapon to force me to divulge information I didn't have, like what all the shooting was about and who was involved. And if I went looking for the information on my own, I was liable to bump into the police investigation I was trying to avoid.

A quick check of the Volvo didn't reveal any obvious bullet holes. I drove to my office, booted up the computer and posted the license numbers I had collected during my adventure. I had posted the BMW's license the morning after it followed me from the Lomax home. The DMV information was waiting in my e-mail. It listed my tail as Alice Marie Hunziger. I didn't think so. I loaded the phone directory CD-ROM and typed in Alice Marie's address, Condon Street in Lawndale.

If ever a place had lost touch with its roots, it was Lawndale. It had started life as two bedroom, one bath bungalows on 40 by 127 lots. No one ever proved zoning bribes, but pretty soon duplexes and two-on-a-lots sprung up. Only the crabgrass on the railroad right of way had survived the onslaught. Some of the houses along Condon were actually built on old right of way, skinny places that looked like single-wide mobile homes. The phone number popped up and I called.

"Hullo?" It was a woman's voice, short of patience and probably accustomed to screaming at the unruly children I could hear in the background.

"Alice Marie Hunziger?"

"Who's this?"

"Are you the owner of a gray BMW coupe?"

She didn't give me a chance to read the license number. "Don't you gimme no shit about that car. That's Davey's. It's just in my name until he gets his ass off probation. I ain't paying no tickets he got on it and I ain't paying no damages he done."

"Davey Hunziger?"

"Davey none of your fucking business." An earful of dial tone made it emphatic.

The directory listing was for a Steven Hunziger, so I ruled out Davey as her husband. That didn't leave me with much. Resident of or visitor at an apartment building that called itself Camelot, probable male relative of Mrs. Alice Marie Hunziger of suburban Lawndale, currently under a probation agreement which forbade his owning a motor vehicle and likely frowned on hijacking as well. I brought up the street map software.

It took three mouse clicks to pinpoint the address where the convoy originated. If the computer wizards ever made finding people that easy, I was out of business. The directory listed an El Camino Enterprises. A recorded phone message confirmed the information in English and Spanish. I declined to leave a message after the beep and killed the rest of the morning doing research.

None of the credit agencies had anything on El Camino. Ditto the Chamber of Commerce, the Better Business Bureau and a raft of local associations. The Secretary of State listed the owner as Hector Simonides. His home phone turned out to be a sushi bar. His address was three blocks out in the Pacific Ocean. The real Mr. Simonides was probably a derelict who had peddled his ID for a jug of T-bird.

I called the business next door to El Camino Enterprises, told the receptionist I was looking for El Camino Roofing Supplies and asked her if that could possibly be the place. She was pretty sure it wasn't. She didn't know exactly what they made, but about a year ago they'd brought in a huge machine that took a week to install.

I played a long shot and called Peter Lomax. "Henry Spain, Mr. Lomax. El Camino Enterprises?"

"You were hired to investigate my mother's background."

The fact he knew the two weren't connected meant he knew something about El Camino. "They have a CD replicating machine," I said.

Silence confirmed my guess.

"You made a point of complaining about software piracy," I reminded him. "I thought I should bring the information to your attention and see if you wanted me to follow up."

"No," he blurted, and then composed himself. "No. Thank you. The matter is being handled." Suddenly he was late for a meeting.

He left me wondering how desperate Prescott was to put the pirates at El Camino out of business. It could have been Peter Lomax, not Paige, who put Davey up to tailing me. I didn't think it was Peter on the other end of Davey's cell phone, setting up the hijacking. That required the kind of savvy picked up at Pelican Bay, not Princeton. But if Lomax's firm was footing the bill, he might have come into contact with Davey, and hired him for a little surveillance on the side when I called with the bad news about his mother.

The phone intruded on my suspicions.

"Henry Spain Investigations."

"This is Officer Enright, Los Angeles Police Department."

Panic came and went. If this was about the hijacking, I'd be looking into multiple gun muzzles, not answering the phone. Best guess: on top of everything else, the Aguilar killing was back.

"What can I do for you?"

"Remain in your office. I'm on my way downtown. I want to talk to you."

I took the elevator down to the lobby cafeteria and bought a barbecued chicken pizza and a pint of milk. Experience had taught me that if I was going into investigative detention, it was best to go on a full stomach. I didn't know if bad breath would discourage prolonged interrogation, but I had nothing to lose finding out.

Enright didn't seem to be in any hurry. I was probably supposed to sweat myself into a simpering pile of cooperation. I was munching distractedly on the last of my pizza while I checked web-sites to see which firms in my industry handled software piracy investigations when he finally arrived. I had the impression I was a late addition to his calendar. His sport coat was buttoned. He was wearing a tie. His after-shave was strong enough to challenge the pizza for aromatic supremacy.

"Please," I said, indicating the two chairs in front of the desk. "Sit down."

He sat carefully to preserve his trouser creases. The vertical stripes in his dress shirt remained parallel, which told me he wasn't carrying a gun. Contrary to TV scripts and department regulations, most police investigators saw service pistols as a nuisance. Their weapon of choice was psychological ambush.

Enright opened his portfolio on his lap and consulted his notes. "You interviewed Brigadier General Franklin Winter yesterday."

He made it sound like a Class A felony, looking me over like I had already been convicted and exhausted my last appeal.

"I'm sorry, I can't discuss that."

"Mr. Spain, you are licensed only as a private investigator. That license gives you no privilege to withhold information from a law enforcement officer."

I handed a photocopy of Paige Lomax's engagement letter across the desk. Enright read it more than once. He was probably scouring his five credit hours of *Introduction to Criminal Law* for something to say about it.

"There is nothing here that would authorize you to interfere in a police investigation."

"I'm not interfering. As stated in the letter from Paige Lomax, which you just read and are welcome to keep as your copy, I'm conducting a civil investigation under the auspices of the attorney of record for an estate."

The desk recorder was running, and I wanted all that on the tape. Enright scowled at my performance. Judging from his wardrobe, he had just returned from Holmby Hills and an interview with a man too rich for him to bully. It was easy to picture him sitting erect in front of the desk, a glaring Major Cole braced at parade rest behind Winter and the old man toying with the polite police officer as he had with me—every question another opportunity for a lecture and the attention that went with it. Enright tucked the letter away in his portfolio.

"Your record indicates you served in Vietnam. Is that correct?"

"Yes."

"Are you familiar with the assassination devices used by the Viet Cong?"

"All I ever saw were North Vietnamese Army regulars. They carried Soviet bloc military weapons."

"I'm talking about a single shot small caliber smoothbore weapon made in the shape of a fountain pen for concealment."

His description sounded like the zip guns we used to make in high school metal shop.

"Is that what killed Eladio Aguilar?"

"Do you think General Winter would be familiar with such a weapon?"

"I've no idea."

"You do see where this is going, don't you, Mr. Spain? A Vietnam era general with a motive for murder. A Vietnam era veteran in the area of a murder probably committed with a Vietnam era weapon."

"You know what I was doing that night."

"A private investigator on routine stakeout witnesses a professional assassination."

"I didn't see anything."

"You saw a woman in a Bentley."

"You've talked to Stephanie St. John."

"How many Bentleys have you seen in your life, Mr. Spain?"

I just shrugged.

"It must be frustrating"—he glanced around the office—"making do with hand-me-down furniture while other entrepreneurs make fortunes."

"I do what I do by choice," I said, but I felt like he could see right through me.

"A steady flow of hush money could set you up for life. It was just a matter of letting Stephanie St. John lead you to someone rich enough to pay off."

I considered him for a minute, wondering whether he was serious, or just throwing a wild theory at me to see what I'd say trying to disprove it.

"You're making it up," I decided. "Winter didn't accuse me of trying to shake him down."

"How could he? Without implying his own guilt?"

"You're kidding, right? Winter condemned me by failing to accuse me."

He ignored the remark to write himself a note. "Do you think the Lomax family might benefit from Alex Sturtevant's death?"

"Killing Sturtevant would dredge up all his old accusations."

"Then you were aware that as an undeclared candidate for the city council Mrs. Lomax might be vulnerable to a suggestion that she extend her lawyer-client privilege to someone investigating Sturtevant."

"Mrs. Lomax suggested the engagement. It's not an investigation of Sturtevant."

"I am going to have her letter reviewed by the Department's counsel."

"Good."

I wasn't happy about the prospect, but I did need to know how solid my ground was. Enright didn't look happy either, probably because he was having a hard time finding anyone who would take his act seriously.

"I offered you a polygraph examination. You refused. Why was that, Mr. Spain?"

"Were other witnesses examined?"

"What does that have to do with your refusal?"

"Why am I being singled out?"

"I'm offering you a chance to clear yourself."

"No law enforcement officer has the authority to clear anyone. If new information came to your attention after I passed a polygraph, you would be legally required to investigate it."

"What information?" Hard words from a man who didn't like being reminded his power had limits.

"Any information."

He closed the zipper case and stood. "Mr. Spain, if you attempt to profit by withholding evidence, you will be found out and you will be punished."

I probably shouldn't have said, "Have a nice day."

He left and I shut off the recorder. Nerves churned my stomach. The remains of my pizza tasted like cardboard. I trashed them and sat brooding.

The good news was that retired Brigadier General Franklin Winter had been promoted to prime suspect in the murder of Eladio Aguilar. I was reduced to extortion and obstruction of justice. The bad news was it wouldn't last. Unless the police had evidence I hadn't heard about, Winter's well-connected attorneys would have a quiet talk with their friends in the power structure and Enright would be told to seek his perpetrator elsewhere.

Elsewhere, in this case, was liable to mean me. If there was evidence against Winter, I needed to chase it down while I was still at large. It was time I found out what actually happened when Cynthia Lomax met the Starliner.

Chapter 16

Gabriel Skidmore wasn't happy when I suggested another visit. I asked if he'd rather talk to the police. He told me he took a nap in the afternoon, but would be awake by four, if I cared to come then. I spent the time calling my list of agencies that investigated software piracy. As ignorant as I was on the subject, all I could do was ask to speak to whoever was handling the El Camino matter. I went through most of them before I found a receptionist who transferred me.

"Grey Mallory speaking."

I had met Mallory once. He was a retired Secret Service agent with executive hair and all the right connections. He was also vice president and regional manager for a prestigious international agency. If he was taking calls personally, El Camino was bigger than I had thought.

"Henry Spain, Mr. Mallory."

"What's this about El Camino, Spain?"

A voice full of managerial bluster left no doubt he remembered our encounter; a skirmish over an insurance bounty. I had nothing to lose being short with him.

"I need to know who's behind it."

"What's your interest?"

I could hear dollar signs in his voice. His vocabulary didn't include the word sharing.

"Unrelated background investigation," I assured him.

"Be specific."

"This is a courtesy call, Mr. Mallory. The idea is to give you a chance to tell me what I need to know so you won't have me underfoot trying to learn it on my own."

"Forget El Camino, Spain. It's out of your league."

"Who is behind it?"

"No, Spain. You're not hearing me. You—"

"They've got mega-buck CD replicating equipment. Who put up the money?"

Mallory's abrupt silence said more than words. I could practically hear him wondering how much I knew and how I came by the information; wanting to ask then realizing his questions might tell me more than my answers told him.

"The financial backing comes from Mexico City. That's all I'm prepared to say."

Likely it was all he knew. Money trails were all but impossible to follow in Mexico. He was probably hoping I'd go chase this one.

"Who can I talk to locally?" I asked. "Who runs the operation here?"

"Don't even think about it, Spain. You're out of the picture. Willful disruption of this investigation will be grounds for a lawsuit."

He hung up and left me nothing to do but wait and see what came back on the license plates I had posted. Maybe I could trade him an ID on the hijackers for more information. He could play hero turning them over to the police, which would get them off my back. Meanwhile I kept a sharp eye on the mirror while I drove out to see Gabriel Skidmore.

Skidmore let me in with a reluctant show of politeness. We sat in his little parlor. The scent of old age closed in around me, oppressive and vaguely sweet. To appearances Skidmore's past hung in the array of photographs on the wall, moments of time frozen in silver nitrate. Reality lay on a coffee table, a newspaper open to yesterday's funeral announcements.

"I wish I could have come under better circumstances," I said.

"Please have some respect for my intelligence, Mr. Spain. You didn't come to offer condolences."

I wanted to tell him the condolences were pure even if my motives weren't, but what I had in mind would probably work better if I left my ogre suit on.

"I missed you at the service."

"I wasn't invited. To Ramona, I was never more than an intruder."

"You were an intruder by anyone's definition. A voyeur stalking an actress."

"Never with malice." Skidmore began rocking; a sad, peaceful man who had just seen another piece of his life slip away. "Only with the foolish hope of a young man."

"You're no longer young, or foolish, so let's stop playing games."

"Excuse me?" His eyes filled with quiet indignation.

"You learned more than you told me the last time we talked."

"I answered you truthfully. You saw my surveillance notes."

"I asked if you recognized any of the men with Sigrid Helstrom when she raided the Caliente Beach Club."

"I did not," he assured me.

"I asked the wrong question."

He stopped rocking.

"I should have asked if you knew today who any of them were."

Relief flickered in his features, as if he had feared worse, and tension drained away into the mocking serenity of superior knowledge.

"If I have withheld information from the police all these years, it would be foolish to give it to you now."

"Ramona sent me to you to learn the truth."

"Ramona couldn't have known how much I knew." His voice fell. "She wouldn't have cared."

"She expected you to tell me something, or she wouldn't have let your name slip."

"But you are only guessing what it might be."

"Let's start with the obvious," I said. "If you kept quiet about the Caliente Beach Club to protect Ramona, you also would have tried to identify the men involved to make sure they didn't pose a threat to her."

Skidmore rocked peacefully and said nothing.

"One of the men was a professional trucker, wasn't he?"

I was guessing that Sigrid had used her old gang to meet the Starliner. She would have needed a heavy truck to move the gold. That meant an eighteen-wheel license, preferably in the pocket of a man who wouldn't stick at murder if the party got rough.

"Wasn't he?" I insisted.

"What difference could it possibly make?"

Telling him about the Starliner wouldn't get me anywhere. Rogue American officers and tons of contraband gold were part of an alien white world. I had to reach him on a personal level.

"You're a moral man. You know this has to be set right. The book has to be closed."

I wasn't sure whether I was appealing to his conscience or his pride. Maybe it was the combination that stopped his rocking again and left him solemn.

"The man who drove the DeSoto was the only one I ever identified."

"How did you find him?"

"Quite by accident," he said. "As a Negro, I was low man on the studio security totem pole. One evening when a member of the uniformed staff called in sick, I had to fill in on the delivery gate. I recognized one of the drivers bringing a load of lights back from a location shoot. I hadn't seen him before because he wasn't a studio employee. He worked for a contract trucking firm."

"But that night you were in a position to check his license and verify his identity."

Skidmore nodded. "His name was Benjamin Neiborsky."

"Where can I find him?"

"I don't know if he's still alive."

That was a problem. Sigrid and Ramona were already dead and given the time that had passed, the actuarial odds were against me. I needed more than one name.

"You were a thorough investigator. You checked on him. Followed him. Tried to learn who the others were."

"When I had the opportunity."

"And?"

Skidmore shook his head. "I never saw him contact anyone I recognized from the Caliente Beach Club."

"You were also watching Sigrid Helstrom for Malcolm Trevor."

"None of the gang ever went near her."

I had to admit that was possible. Maybe even likely. If Trevor had confronted Sigrid about the Beach Club, she would have known she'd been followed and been very careful from there on. And if Ramona knew Skidmore was doing the following, Sigrid knew it as well.

Skidmore's reedy voice had sounded a bit strained, but mine probably would too if I managed to live as long as he had. His bony hands rested easily on the chair arms, with no tension or tremor to suggest he was lying. He was just a man weighed down by the weariness of seven decades and the loss of a treasured dream.

"How is your health?" I asked.

He gave me a surprised look. "I'm well enough, thank you, all things considered."

"I ask because there could be other investigators following this trail soon. They may be hostile."

A poignant smile touched his lips. "Perhaps Ramona's passing was merciful."

"Are you going to hold up all right?"

He took a minute to consider the question. "I suppose I could be charged as an accessory."

"The authorities have enough African American community relations problems without digging up a crime that's older than cave dirt. You'll probably get off with a tongue lashing from a deputy prosecutor. But you will have to tell them everything. Even the things you've kept from me. Perhaps especially those things."

"You are a cynic, Mr. Spain."

It wasn't a criticism, just a bland statement of fact. As if I weren't human, but some instrument of divine intervention sent to strip him of the ill-gotten peace he was enjoying in his declining years.

I thought about General Franklin Winter, living out his last years in an exotic mausoleum in Holmby Hills. In World War II, he had been an officer cavorting in nightclubs while Gabriel Skidmore had been a Private taking pictures for the Army Public Information Office. Today they differed only in their surroundings. Two forgotten men clinging to their pride and their memories. Both were harboring secrets. Maybe the same secrets. I had no clue. I didn't even know what questions to ask to get at them.

"Whatever you did or didn't do may have been justified in the context of the times," I told Skidmore, "but the times and the context have changed."

"I learned nothing more about the Caliente Beach Club robbery. I was one man with little training and few resources."

"And about the things you haven't told me?"

"I will make my peace with God, Mr. Spain."

I didn't have an argument for that, so I thanked him and left to fight the evening commute back downtown. My computer made short work of the phone directory and turned up a Benjamin Neiborsky in Gardena.

On the way I stopped at a steak house for a solid dinner, a stiff Cuba Libre and a little thinking time before I tried my luck. I knew my chances of learning what I needed to know lay entirely in technique.

Conceptually the situation was simple. All I had to do was knock on Neiborsky's door, introduce myself and ask him whether he had known Sigrid Helstrom, and if he had would he please be so kind as to fess up to his involvement in several murders.

Chapter 17

The house stood on Patronella, a little down from Cerise, in a blue collar neighborhood built about the time the Benjamin Neiborsky I was looking for would have come into money. The yard light showed a two tone '59 Ranchero in the car port; a retired trucker's pride and joy. Except for the bark of a dog that didn't take kindly to strangers, the evening was still. Television noise came faintly through Neiborsky's front door. Who and how many were inside I couldn't know. I thumbed the buzzer and waited.

The noise faded. The January chill sent a graveyard shiver through me. I gave my first serious thought to the possible consequences of tracking down a killer who had eluded the police for half a century.

The man who opened the door was past seventy, tall and flat-chested in a rumpled T-shirt. Most of his strength seemed to be in long, thick arms matted with gray hair. More gray hair was slicked back at the sides of a bald head to make a fifties DA. He peered at me, like he had never really gotten used to wearing glasses and didn't quite trust anything he saw through them.

Who're you?" Between the slur in his voice and the fragrance of his breath, he'd already gone through at least a six pack.

"My name's Henry Spain, Mr. Neiborsky."

"Whadda you wan?"

"I'd like to talk to you about Sigrid Helstrom."

He tried to shut the door. My shoe was in the way.

"Get outta here!" he bellowed.

"Or what? You'll call the police?"

"Fuckin' A."

"Go ahead," I said. "If they don't want to hear about The Shadows, there's always the Caliente Beach Club."

A belch rose and startled him out of his belligerence. I had his attention. It was time to make my pitch.

"I'm a private investigator, Mr. Neiborsky. I don't care what you've done. I don't want to hurt you. I just need some information."

"Yeah?"

"Why don't you invite me in for a beer? We can have a little chat, and I'll be on my way."

He wasn't enthusiastic about the idea, but he didn't seem to have a better one handy. He let me in and locked the door against any friends I might have lurking outside.

The living room was presentable in the Spartan style of men who lived alone. A few feminine knick-knacks left on the shelving suggested he was a widower. He sank down in a recliner. The television was still on. Images flickered without sound. He hoisted a beer bottle and took a pull.

I helped myself to a seat on a faded sofa. "You met Sigrid Helstrom on the studio lot, didn't you?"

Wind came in a soft rush. Flatulence drifted on the air. Neiborsky smiled. "Me and a lot of guys. So what?"

"But you were the one she picked to drive when she took down The Shadows."

"Says who?"

"Relax, will you? If I wanted you arrested, the police would have been here hours ago."

"You're playing some kind of angle."

"Sure I am. It's called earning a living."

He gave me some more scrutiny.

"Why did Sigrid pick you?" I asked.

"What's it to you?"

"Look, Neiborsky, I haven't got all night. Talk to me or talk to the law."

"You got no proof."

"Try an eyewitness."

I gave him Skidmore's version of how he'd hot wired the Delgado Inn's DeSoto and driven to the Caliente Beach Club. His eyes went from nervous to worried to scared.

"Why did Sigrid pick you?" I repeated.

"She knew I was in the war," he said sullenly. "She knew I drove for a living."

"How did you meet her?"

"I seen her at the studio. Tried chatting her up. First she cold shoulders me and then out of the blue she tells me to meet her for a drink."

"But she had business in mind."

"She showed up with this guy called Farmer. They put the deal to me. Did I want to handle the wheel for a share in a job?"

"Tell me about Farmer."

"He was trouble."

"What kind of trouble?"

"Trouble." As if anyone with a brain would know.

"Where did Sigrid find him?"

"Some movie she was in. Motorcycle racing. Farmer, he rode the dirt track circuit. They shot some scenes there."

"Why did she pick him?"

"I dunno. Bad rep, I suppose."

"Tell me about it."

"He wore these overalls when he rode. Made like he was a hick. Just waiting for somebody to smart off so he could punch them out. Carried a sawed-off in his saddlebag."

"Farmer handled the shotgun at The Shadows? Sigrid used the pistol?"

"I didn't see none of that. I sat around the corner with the engine idling. When I heard the shotgun go, I came in fast. Sig and Farmer piled in and I burned rubber."

Neiborsky fortified himself with another slug of beer.

"Sounds like easy money, don't it? Well, it wasn't. All day before the job, I couldn't crap. I'd go to the john and nothing. That night, sitting there alone, I was so scared I could have puked. I was in the war. Normandy all the way across the Rhine. It wasn't the same. In the war, you was with guys you knew. Guys you could trust. That night it was just a couple people I only talked to a few times. It wasn't the same."

"But you came back for a return engagement at the Caliente Beach Club."

"Sig bugged me about it for more'n a year. She was crazy about it, that's what she was."

"Why did you go along?"

"I blew the cash from the first job. Bought me a new Hudson. New threads. Broads. Parties. Trip to Reno. Just farted it away. I figured I'd be smarter the second time around. I'd take one more big risk and be set for life."

"It took five of you to raid the Beach Club."

"That was Sig's big thing. She had this certain way it hadda be done. We hadda get two more guys. Me and Farmer, we each hadda get one guy apiece."

"Which guy was yours?"

"I didn't know no crooks, so I hit Bunny up about it."

"Bunny?"

"Sodawasser. He was my Lieutenant in the war. Normandy all the way across the Rhine. Nobody could shoot a Carbine like Bunny. I seen him in action plenty, so I knew his nerve was good." Neiborsky drank some more beer and eyed me closely. "Hey, I thought you knew about all this?"

"Did Sigrid make any comment about his being an officer? A Lieutenant?"

"Yeah," he recalled dimly. "Only it wasn't nothing she said. It was the way she looked at me. Like when she was asking me where I knew him from. She was different. Nothing I could put my finger on. Just different."

Details were coming back out of the haze of time. Little things that still bothered him. He looked to me for an explanation. I didn't give him one, but even secret knowledge was enough to re-establish my bonafides.

"They hit it off all right when I brought him around," he went on. "Bunny was a bookkeeper. Quiet type. Brains and culture. Sig really got off on that crap."

I remembered Malcolm Trevor. "Any particular reason?"

"Sig was dirt, just like Farmer and me, and she hated it. She didn't want nothing to do with us outside the jobs. Fucking social climber. That's what she was."

That tied in with her marriage to Harold Lomax. "Bunny drove her to the Beach Club?"

"They was supposed to pretend they was making out. Pretend, my ass. Sig stuck her tits against him and had herself a party. Bunny, he was trying to be a gentleman, not getting too personal the way he held her. She just shoved his hand down where she wanted it."

"There was a fourth man at—"

"I bet she give him some," he grumbled and scratched an armpit.

"Who was the fourth man?"

"Never give me none, but I bet she give him some. That son of a bitch."

Neiborsky drained his beer and found another in a holder on the carpet next to his chair. I gave him a minute to pry it open.

"The fourth man?"

"Guy's name was Mickey something."

"Mickey who?"

"Mickey Mouse for all I know. Him and Farmer took out the bagman. Sig and Bunny creamed the wheelman. All I done was drive the DeSoto."

"But you got a full share," I said.

"One fifth of one hundred eighty four thousand smacks," Neiborsky told me proudly. "Got married on that cash. Bought this place."

I didn't tell him that was probably a short count. Ramona Benitez had been taken care of somehow. And Sigrid wouldn't have known she would need Neiborsky and his commercial trucker's license again in twenty odd years.

"How much did you get when you met the airplane in the desert?" I asked, trying to sound nonchalant while sweat tickled my spine. The Starliner was the reason I had come. If Neiborsky hadn't been involved, I was at a dead end.

"That was a whole different thing," he said. "Sig never planned to do that guy. He come, like, right out of nowhere."

I felt my fingers dig into the arm of the sofa. If Sigrid had killed someone collecting the gold from the Starliner, the charge would be felony murder. It would apply equally to everyone involved in the conspiracy. The penalty could be life and there would be no statute of limitations. General Winter would be as vulnerable today as he was a quarter of a century ago. I fought down the urge to start firing questions at Neiborsky. He could clam up any time, and there would be nothing I could do about it. My best shot was to keep pretending I knew pretty much everything already, and had just dropped by to check a few stray facts.

"What kind of truck did you use?"

"Sig tells me to go to this rental place. Everything's arranged. Flatbed and a forklift to go with it."

"The five of you met the plane?"

"Sucker was huge. Four engines. Noise like you wouldn't believe. You could feel the air shake when it got close. I didn't think the pilot could land it on that little strip, but he put it down slicker than greased owl shit. Kicked up a fucking sandstorm when he reversed the propellers. We had to climb in the trucks to keep from choking."

"More than one truck," I supplied, "because part of the cargo was going to Phoenix and part was staying in L.A."

"I don't know from Phoenix. Sig rented a van for some of it. The rest she told me drive to Berdoo. I locked the flatbed in this warehouse and never seen it again."

Sigrid had been too smart to deliver to the mob in Phoenix. She had deducted the smugglers' cut and locked the rest in a warehouse in San Bernardino for the bad boys to pick up.

"Did you know what you were hauling?"

"Five grand for five hours work. That's all I hadda know."

"That's not much to risk a murder charge."

"That wasn't Sig's fault. Weirdo just showed up in that silly ass yellow jeep. Him and that broad."

I didn't like the way the story was developing, but I didn't dare let my worry show. "Look, nobody's blaming you. I just need to get all the details straight."

"The dumb shit kept asking us what we were doing," Neiborsky said, rebelling at the stupidity of it. "We told him to move along, but he wasn't hearing it. I figure maybe he was cranked up on speed or something. I mean, the pilot was revving up to take off and this yo-yo ran out in front of the plane yelling at him to stop, like anyone could hear him over the engines. The propellers were turning so fast they were just a blur. Farmer and Mickey hadda wrestle the dumb fuck out of the way so he don't get sliced and diced."

"Was he armed?"

"The jerk grabbed Mickey's gun. What could Sig do? A head case like that, he could've killed someone. She hadda take him off."

"What about the woman with him?"

Neiborsky leered off into space, as if he could see her still. "Blonde. Nice and young. What's that word—nubile? Could have had us a party with her, but Sig wouldn't hear it." He looked at me, wondering if I might know why. "Mickey just mentioned it, and Sig lit into him. I never seen her go off like that."

"What did she do with the woman?"

"Farmer used to make cycle trips to Mexico. Carrying weight, if you know what I mean. Said he knew a place he could sell her. Sig didn't like that much either, but none of us wanted to whack her."

Sigrid's dilemma raised the possibility of a second witness. "Did you happen to get either of their names?"

A hiccup startled Neiborsky. He peered at me suddenly and sharply, as if he couldn't quite remember how I had wound up on his sofa, then retrieved a fresh beer and tossed it in my general direction.

"Suck on that a minute. I gotta take a leak."

He heaved himself up from the recliner and padded out of the room, disappearing down a hall on his urgent mission. I stood up and put the beer back. The noiseless flicker of the TV caught my eye. It was another relic of the fifties, Alfred Hitchcock's *North By Northwest.* The ersatz crop-duster biplane was coming in low over a cornfield to machine gun Cary Grant at a lonely intersection. I switched it off.

My brain had hit overload. Neiborsky had given me more information than I could absorb in one sitting. I was simultaneously trying to come up with more questions to ask him and ways to check what he had already said when I became aware too much time had passed. I hadn't heard a door close, or any tinkle of water. Survival instinct had me headed down the hall before I had time to think.

Neiborsky was coming the other way. We collided. He stumbled against the wall. If it hadn't been for that, I wouldn't have had time to block his gun. It went off against my coat sleeve and sent pain searing through my arm. I kicked Neiborsky in the shin. He let out a yell. I bent his arm behind his head and twisted the gun from his fingers. He was off balance when I released him. He landed on his backside. I stood over him on wobbly legs with my ears ringing from the shot. The pistol in my hand was a snub-nosed .22 revolver called a Banker's Special. Colt hadn't made that model for sixty years. This one looked its age. I didn't want to think about how many scores it might have settled.

Neiborsky glared up at me. "Gimme my Goddamn piece."

"So you can shoot me?" I snarled.

"You know too fucking much."

He had been playing me, telling me his story to check my knowledge. I had been playing him, pretending I already knew most of it to keep him talking. Two cretins trying to outwit each other.

He came unsteadily to his feet. "Give it over or I'm going for my shotgun."

I spun on my heel and got out of there. I wasn't worried about the shotgun. I was afraid of what I might do to Neiborsky if I stuck around. I could practically see the six point screamer headlines: *Retiree Slain By Home Invader. Local man in custody.*

Adrenaline coursed through my system as I hoofed it out to my car. I didn't hear any sirens. No neighbors put their heads out for a look. The quiet pop of Neiborsky's .22 had gone unnoticed.

I opened the trunk of the Volvo, wrapped the pistol in a rag and stuck it in the toolbox. The last thing I needed was to get busted for concealed carry.

I was able to drive all right, but my arm wouldn't stop leaking blood. I got my coat off at a stoplight and tried to use my handkerchief. It didn't help much. I was getting light headed.

CHAPTER 18

"Does this happen often?"

Cassandra Freegate wrung a thin soup of blood and hot water out of a washcloth into the kitchen sink. Her minivan had been in the driveway when I found my way home.

"Only when I do really stupid things," I said through clenched teeth.

Neiborsky's bullet had cut along the flesh from just above my elbow half way up to my shoulder, exposing more nerve endings than I knew I had in my entire body. I got the full impact when Cassandra started dabbing antiseptic.

"Hold still," she ordered.

"Where did you learn medicine? From Jack the Ripper?"

"On the job training. Both my brothers and most of my boyfriends liked to fight. They brought home all sorts of little souvenirs. Now pretend you're trying to impress me how tough you are and shut up."

I decided I'd better put a cork in it before she told me to do the job myself.

"You're lucky it was just a .22," she said.

I didn't think luck had anything to do with it. Neiborsky had probably chosen the Banker's Special to finish me off with a quiet shot to the head so he could get rid of the body with the neighbors none the wiser.

Cassandra unrolled cotton along the wound and secured it with tape. "You could have stopped at a fire station, you know. They have real medics there."

"They have to report gunshot wounds."

She gave me a worried look. "Are you in trouble?"

"If you'll make the drinks, I'll tell you about it."

In the bedroom I found a zip-front cardigan I could put on without moving my right arm. I didn't expect it to help much. The chill in my bones probably had more to do with blood loss than room temperature. A Cuba Libre was waiting on the bar when I got to the rec room. I took a stiff belt to wash down a couple of aspirin.

Cassandra had curled up at one end of the sofa to nibble on a glass of scotch. The letterman's jacket was pulled tight around her shoulders like armor. Nothing in her posture invited intimacy so I sat at the other end and tried to read whatever else her body language was saying.

I wasn't sure what I was looking for. Maybe it was just male insecurity. Men liked to dream about getting lucky with a hot chick, but if it actually happened, there were always nagging suspicions about hidden agendas. I already had a few doubts about Cassandra. Her husband had insisted I go into East L.A. to look for her son. An Anglo like Robbie Freegate had no reason to buy grass in East L.A. High school pushers sold it out of their backpacks and lockers. And the quiet corner Jerry Freegate steered me to didn't fit the drug scene. No dealers. No Friday night traffic. Not even left-over gang graffiti.

"What exactly did the neighbor girl's parents tell you about Robbie's shopping trip to East L.A.?" I asked.

Mention of her son got her attention. "Jerry talked to them. He wouldn't even tell me who they were. He said I didn't know them." She gave me an embarrassed smile. "He's sort of protective."

In my paranoid state it sounded more like evasive. Jerry Freegate was a Berkut and Schroeder client. Paige Lomax was a partner in the firm. I wondered if there was a connection. I told Cassandra about meeting Stevie and tracing the Bentley she was driving to Harold Lomax. Cassandra had no reaction to the Lomax name. I told her about Peter Lomax hiring me to check his mother's background; about my interview with Ramona Benitez. She arched her eyebrows when I got to New Year's Eve at The Shadows.

"Raped in a nightclub?"

"By all accounts, yes."

"Nightclubs are packed on New Year's Eve."

She was accustomed to uptown and swanky. I'd conjured up a mental picture of tawdry neon, cigarette haze and a cheap dance band in an out-of-the-way spot the police were paid to ignore. The L.A. of Buggsy Seigel and Mickey Cohen.

"Places like The Shadows had cozy little rooms tucked away in the back."

"Why would Sigrid and Ramona go to that kind of club? I thought the idea was to meet important movie people."

"They were at the bottom of the food chain. Anyone with a studio pass probably seemed important to them."

"So where did the five Army officers come from?"

I had no answer for that; just Ramona's accusation, Franklin Winter's admission and Sigrid's revenge to make it fact. I told Cassandra about the robbery of The Shadows and the raid on the Caliente Beach Club, both committed on New Year's Eve and both done according to the script of *Ambush Road.* I didn't know why I told her, except that I had her interest and wanted to keep it. Her increasingly skeptical expression had me thoroughly defensive by the time I finished.

"I know it sounds like a crock, but it happened."

"I thought Sigrid was trying to charm her way into the movies."

"She did."

I told Cassandra about Malcolm Trevor, not really understanding how a downtrodden film doctor could sponsor careers for two actresses, just telling the tale as it was told to me.

"Then what were the two robberies about? If she had what she wanted, why risk screwing it up? And why wait so long?"

"Human nature. People get what they want, wallow in it for a while then start taking it for granted and wanting more."

I told her Alex Sturtevant's tale of contraband gold whisked out of Saigon and Neiborsky's version of what happened when Sigrid met the Starliner in California. All I got for my trouble was a look of horror.

"Do you think they really sold that poor woman in Mexico?"

"I don't know."

All I had to go on was an alcohol sodden recollection of something that happened a quarter of a century ago. And even that assumed Neiborsky wasn't just feeding me a line of bull to test the limits of my knowledge. I was wandering in the frustrating twilight that sometimes settles over an investigation, where there's too much corroboration to blow off what you've heard, but what you do have doesn't make sense as it stands.

Cassandra read my mind. "More holes than cheese?"

"Don't be flippant. I'm supposed to be clever enough to do this sort of thing for a living."

"Shouldn't you tell the police?"

"I'm working for a lawyer. Anything I learn is legally part of what is called attorney work product. It's protected under attorney-client privilege."

"But what if that woman is still alive somewhere in Mexico?"

That was a question I didn't want to face until I absolutely had to. I fortified myself with ninety proof confidence.

"I'll find her."

Cassandra's dubious look said more than words.

"I found Robbie, didn't I? How is he doing, by the way?"

"You were right about Jerry being my best shot."

I knew from the way she looked at me that we weren't talking about Robbie. "It wasn't a coincidence you were sitting in my driveway when I got home, was it?"

She gave her head a quick shake; a tense little movement that amplified the nervousness in her eyes. An apologetic smile came suddenly. Words tumbled from her mouth, like one of those carefully thought out speeches people sometimes blurt out helter skelter under stress.

"You have to dance with the guy who brought you to the prom. It's one of the main rules. Anyway, what I came to say is that I won't be around anymore."

She drained her scotch to make it official.

"Jerry is your best shot," I admitted, more to myself than Cassandra.

As the years passed, Jerry Freegate would grow wealthier and more prominent. Henry Spain would just grow older. Even that would require luck. I had already let myself get shot by an over-the-hill drunk. I didn't want to think about what could happen if I ran across someone really dangerous.

Cassandra stood up and put her empty glass on the bar. "We're too much alike, you and me. We're both lost in worlds we don't understand. We need to attach ourselves to someone with a sense of direction."

"Well, thanks for the medical attention."

I stood up too quickly. The combination of liquor and blood loss tried to lift my head off my shoulders. I heard Cassandra ask, "Are you all right?" as the fog cleared.

"Sure. Just a little woozy. I'll be okay. It's Friday. I've got the weekend to recuperate."

That covered my physical condition, but it didn't begin to answer the question. She was right when she called me a lost soul. She was one of the few people who had ever noticed, or bothered to bring up the subject. She was someone I could talk to even if we weren't an item. But her expression told me not to bother raising the possibility.

"Look," she began tentatively, "Jerry's kind of possessive, and—"

She broke off and I knew she had screwed up her courage and come in person to look me in the eye and find out whether I intended to make trouble for her.

"I won't mention anything," I promised. "Or make a nuisance of myself."

She put out a hand. "Well, good-bye."

We shook on it and she left. I stood in the doorway, watching helplessly until her taillights were gone. There had been nothing suspicious or sinister in our fling. Robbie's disappearance had destabilized her comfortable life. She had reached out for something reassuring. I happened to be handy.

Henry Spain, one night stand. My pride hurt, my head throbbed and my arm ached. Feeling sorry for myself wasn't getting me anywhere, so I went back into the kitchen to clean up.

A re-weaver could probably salvage my suit coat, but Neiborsky's attempt to silence me had reduced one of my better shirts to lawn mowing attire. His story had done even more damage. If it were true, it made General Franklin Winter party to the death of a man in the California desert, which provided motivation to support the police theory that he was behind the attempted murder of Alex Sturtevant, which in turn had resulted in the death of Eladio Aguilar.

The first order of business Monday would be to see if I could corroborate what Neiborsky had told me. If I could, then I'd have to weigh the dangers of double crossing Paige Lomax against the perils of withholding information in an active homicide investigation.

CHAPTER 19

By Monday my arm had a scab that itched relentlessly and threatened to rip loose at anything close to my normal range of motion. After three failed Windsor knots I decided to go with a sport coat and an open collar dress shirt. Clothing ads called that business casual. The mirror said cheap hoodlum.

The morning commute gave me time to replay Neiborsky's confession on the micro-cassette recorder. When I got to the office I started making calls to track down any witnesses who might be able to discredit some or all of it.

Albert 'Bunny' Sodawasser had belonged to the VFW until his death last year. Since I was a card-carrying member, they gave me the married name of a surviving daughter who lived in Sausalito. She thought it was wonderful that her father might be included in an article about veterans adjusting to society in the years following World War II. She suggested I talk to her Godmother, who had introduced her parents.

"We've lost touch, but I think she still lives in L.A. She knew my father forever. Her name is Cynthia Lomax."

Strike one.

The curator of a local motorcycle museum had raced from 1948 to 1953. He remembered Farmer, whose true name was Elmer Upshaw. Upshaw was a daring rider who found the money for new equipment in 1950 and made a show in the standings. The curator didn't remember anyone named Mickey, although there had been a freelance track mechanic named Corrigan who was called the Mick. Neither man had shown up for the 1952 season.

Strike two.

Another pilgrimage to the library microfiche reader told me that two days before Sigrid's gang had met the Starliner, a law student had taken his girl friend exploring in the desert on spring college break. When they didn't turn up for class the next week, a search was launched. Only their abandoned Jeep was found.

Strike three.

I went back to the office to call Roy Lee Exum before I made a reluctant trip to the police.

"You were going to check on New Year's Eve 1944 at The Shadows," I reminded her after she had poured the usual ice water over my opening attempt at pleasantry.

"It's going to cost you."

"What is?"

"A look at several photographs. Taken at The Shadows on the evening in question."

"Photographs?" My voice had more disbelief than I had intended.

"A fascinating tidbit of history for you. In those days most night clubs had photographers who paid for a concession to take pictures on festive occasions. They would photograph each table and try to sell the pictures to the people there. Naturally they tried to get anyone they could in a shot with a Hollywood name, if any showed up. We have thousands in our archives, all filed by date."

"I need to see what you found."

"What have you got to trade?"

"Things are getting out of hand. Your pictures may have to go to the police."

"I don't think so." Her tone informed me that she wasn't rolling over for any cheap bluff.

I told her the whole story, partly to listen for things I should leave out when I regurgitated it for the law, partly to see how it played with a professional researcher who was familiar with the period. She was generally unimpressed, and particularly skeptical of Gabriel Skidmore.

"Studios didn't really start integrating until well into the fifties, and it was painful even then. I don't see them trusting an African American to follow a white actress. A gate guard, maybe, or someone to keep the domestic help in line, but no more."

"Malcolm Trevor trusted him."

"Your view of Trevor comes entirely from Ramona Benitez. She was a child of migrant illegals; a US Citizen only because she happened to be born in the Imperial Valley. She ran away at sixteen and arrived in Hollywood barely literate. A man of Trevor's sophistication would have seemed like a god to her. She is not a reliable source when it comes to his true position in the grand scheme of things."

The good news was that Roy Lee had been interested enough interview Ramona's family. "Ramona didn't invent Trevor's Bentley," I reminded her. "Or the fact that *Confidential* magazine was hot on his trail. What do your photos show?"

"Just some people at a party. Not a high crime or misdemeanor in sight."

"Okay, I'll keep you out of it if I possibly can. If you haven't heard from the police in the next couple of hours, you probably won't."

"Call me if you get away in time to buy lunch. I'll bring the pictures."

"It's a date."

I sounded more certain than I felt, but I was encouraged. Roy Lee had taken what I'd said seriously enough to want to pursue it. And she had given me a fresh lead. It took a couple of calls to locate Marisol at work.

"I need to see your grand-mother's photographs from The Shadows on New Year's Eve, 1944."

"You mean when that Sigrid woman was—had her experience?"

"It's important, Marisol. Can you get them for me?"

"I don't know if there are any."

"Could you look, please?"

I gave her my mailing address, promised to take good care of the photos and return them as soon as I could. I had to keep the conversation brief. A woman had just barged into the office.

Even in three-inch heels she was short. A stiff white jacket and tight red skirt did their best to make her look thirty again. Strawberry blonde hair put an incendiary edge on the pouty expression of someone who would keep insisting until she got what she wanted. She came straight to the desk and glared at me.

"Are you Henry Spain?"

I stood up, smiled and waved a hand at the visitors' chairs. "Please, sit down."

"I want you to stop harassing me."

She was serious. Of course, that didn't mean much. After Berkeley, L.A. was the strangest place in California. The fruit loops came in all shapes and sizes. It wasn't unheard of for them to wander into sixth floor offices.

"Madam, I don't even know your name."

"You know I'm Donna Mason."

"Perhaps you've confused me with someone else."

"Nathaniel hired you to spy on me."

Nathaniel was the crime buff I had asked about the Caliente Beach Club. Donna Mason was apparently the romantic problem he had wanted me to solve. She wasn't the streamlined heartbreaker I had pictured.

"Nathaniel did not hire me."

"You went to Camelot."

I had followed someone named Davey to an apartment building named Camelot just before I wound up in the middle of an attempt to hijack a load of pirate software. But I hadn't left my name.

"How do you know I was there?"

"Just because Ernesto was in prison, doesn't mean he doesn't deserve a second chance. He paid his debt to society. You can't persecute him."

I remembered what Alice Marie Hunziger had said about Davey being on probation. My brain dropped into gear with a sudden lurch.

"Camelot is a half-way house, isn't it?"

"You're stalking me. I can get a restraining order against you."

She was David. I was Goliath. She tapped her foot impatiently, waiting for me to realize I had been vanquished.

"Ms. Mason, let us assume for the sake of discussion that everything you say is true. Let us further assume that I promise to repent. When you walk out that door, you will still face the same dilemma you faced when you walked in, won't you?"

Her face turned redder than her hair.

"Wouldn't it be simpler to discuss the situation with Nathaniel?"

"Just leave me alone!"

She turned and slammed out. Precise, angry footsteps took her away down the hall. I sat down and pressed out a phone number. Normally when Nathaniel was in a meeting, I just left a message. This time I had them pull him out.

"My dear Sheerluck, I don't mind talking to you when I have a free minute. In fact, I enjoy it. But right now I'm in conference with—"

"Donna Mason paid me a visit."

"Oh, God!"

"You may want something a little more practical than divine intervention. She's turning out for an ex-con named Ernesto."

I could hear the breath leave him. "Do you kick all your friends between the legs, or am I special?"

"This is no time for sensitivity. Ernesto lives in a halfway house called Camelot. Ever hear of it?"

"Supervised work release for felony offenders."

"Rehabilitation not withstanding, people in that situation are liable to be a couple cans short of a six pack. You need to use whatever contacts you have in the criminal justice system to get a rundown on this character. And a recent picture, so you'll recognize him if he turns up in your rear view."

"I appreciate your concern, but that's out of the question."

"Donna is not your main issue. There'll be other chicks if she walks. You have only one life."

"You don't understand, Henry. People in the corrections system are a protected class. When the State takes custody of them, it assumes responsibility for protecting their persons and privacy. The system also has a vested interest in helping their clients—which is what they're called nowadays—put their pasts behind them and get on with useful lives."

So much for my chances of having him get a line on Davey while he was at it. "Did you tell Donna you were thinking of having her checked out?"

"Certainly not."

"You didn't feel a twinge of guilt? Fess up to our little conversation?"

"Henry, I have no idea why Donna confronted you. If I mentioned you, it was only in passing."

That was probably enough. Donna had a secret. Any mention of an investigator would set off alarm bells.

Educated guess: jailyard eyes inside Camelot spotted me following Davey, who added my name to the grapevine. Ernesto mentioned it to Donna over the weekend and she jumped to the obvious conclusion. At least the timing was right. She had stormed in during Monday morning coffee break, her first logical opportunity to take me to task.

"How many residential work release locations are there in L.A.?" I asked, wondering how Davey and Ernesto wound up in the same building.

"Corrections wants more, but nobody wants one in their back yard."

"Do you know anything about the pro bono parole case Paige Lomax is working on? I think his name is Victor Bradley."

"Is he at Camelot?"

"I don't know. What's his story?"

"It's a fairly well known case from eight or nine years ago. Bradley was just out of high school at the time. Another boy claimed Bradley ran a teenage burglary ring. Two members of the ring killed a homeowner who surprised them. Bradley had an alibi for the time of the killing. The State's corroboration was about as flimsy as it could be and still get the case into court. Of course, trivia like that never bothered a California jury. They convicted Bradley of felony murder."

Felony murder again. Fate was hell-bent on reminding me that Brigadier General Franklin Winter could be prosecuted for a death in the California desert even though he had been in Saigon at the time.

Nathaniel had to get back to his meeting.

I had to get to the police. If Victor Bradley was a resident at Camelot, then Paige Lomax might have been behind the attempt to hijack El Camino. Not only would her engagement letter not protect me, but if the law ever connected her with a felony, it could make me look like an accessory.

I had tried to outwit the system and wound up outwitting myself. Now it was a foot race to the confessional. And I'd have to be damn careful what I said when I got there.

CHAPTER 20

Enright sat me down in a claustrophobic interview room where a video camera in a corner just under the ceiling could record every nervous tic and nuance of voice. Enright was suitably pressed and starched for his appearance; notice to any supervisor who reviewed the tape that he was ready for the next step up the ladder. He gave the camera a case number, told it who was present and had me answer a few questions to assure it I had come of my own free will and hadn't been promised anything or threatened in any way.

The trap was set.

I limited my statement to the saga of Sigrid Helstrom, aka Cynthia Lomax, from her first encounter with General Winter on New Year's Eve, 1944, to her role in the transfer of Winter's contraband gold in 1975. I played my tape of Neiborsky's confession to back it up.

Enright's scowl deepened as he read over his notes. "Do you know what's wrong with this, Mr. Spain?"

"I'm required by law to report all information about crimes to the police, regardless of my opinion of it."

"Each corroborating witness was referred to you by the witness he was corroborating. You haven't found any independent source to verify what they told you."

I had come to tell the story, not sell it, so I didn't argue. Enright didn't like that. He was trying to rile me.

"The Lomax money is alleged to have questionable origins. That could make the family a target for extortion, even if Paige Lomax weren't planning to run for public office."

It was the second time he had mentioned extortion and Paige Lomax's City Council candidacy in the same breath. I wondered if he really did have visions of a fast track career dancing behind the shrewd look he was giving me.

"That's a lot to invent on the spur of the moment," I pointed out.

"More likely it was an old scheme they dusted off for another try when you contacted Ramona Benitez."

Surprise left me staring at him.

"Nothing you've told me post-dates the contents of the Sturtevant book," he said.

"Sturtevant never mentioned Cynthia Lomax." He was too wrapped up in his conspiracy theory to bother checking any other possibilities.

"Think about these people," Enright ordered. "Benitez, Skidmore, Neiborsky"—he ticked them off on his fingers like pieces of irrefutable evidence—"all acquaintances of Cynthia Lomax when she was young. But while she went on to wealth and position, they slipped into threadbare obscurity. Envy would be natural. The Sturtevant book, with its accusations against her husband, might have planted the idea she also was vulnerable to extortion."

"Not if she hadn't done anything."

I wasn't getting the message, and frustration put an edge on Enright's voice. "These people remembered lurid crimes. Even saved news clippings. It would be simple to concoct some involvement on the part of Cynthia Lomax and threaten to accuse her if she didn't share her good fortune."

"Her husband was a retired FBI agent. He would have known how to deal with extortionists."

"Friends from her younger days might well have known things she couldn't take to her husband."

Enright's leer was as obnoxious as his after-shave. He was just one of the boys in the locker room; a ready audience for any juicy tidbits I'd picked up. I hadn't mentioned Malcolm Trevor, and didn't plan to.

"Harold Lomax would have noticed any significant dents in the family bank account."

"They probably didn't ask for much. Just a few small payments to avoid the nuisance of more accusations."

"Neiborsky admitted his own participation. You heard it on the tape."

"After listening to it, I'd say Neiborsky just embellished whatever you mentioned. Probably in the drunken belief there was money in it for him when you took the story to the Lomax family."

He sprung the spool out of my recorder and tucked it into a pocket in his portfolio. I didn't like losing it. It was all I had to back up my version of the Neiborsky interview.

"Your theory doesn't explain enough of what happened," I said.

"This," he said, rapping a knuckle on his notes, "is even shorter on explanations. For example, if Cynthia Lomax really had been involved in two major armed robberies, how would she explain her sudden wealth?"

"Is sugar daddy one word or two?"

"There were men involved. They could hardly tell anyone that."

"The men involved weren't the type who bothered answering questions."

Enright sat back and gave me some clinical scrutiny. "I can appreciate, Mr. Spain, that you don't like to admit you've been duped. But what motive, other than extortion, would any of these people have to tell you anything?"

I didn't have an answer. At first, Ramona and Gabriel Skidmore had seemed like harmless senior citizens hungry for attention. But the more I thought about it, the less sense it made. If Ramona wanted credit for her wild youth, why not just tell me about it? Why hand me tantalizing tidbits and send me out with no assurance I'd find anything? If Skidmore wanted credit for solving the Caliente Beach Club, why leave Neiborsky's name out of his original story?

"I don't know their motives," I admitted. "All I have are the things they told me."

"Last time we spoke," he said, "you were invoking lawyer-client privilege to withhold information. Now you're coming forward voluntarily. What changed your mind?"

"Last time we talked, I didn't know about the murder in the desert. Or that there might be a kidnapped woman still alive somewhere in Mexico."

"Then you haven't had a falling out with your employer?"

"No." But I could definitely see one coming.

"You are aware that all statements you make are subject to investigation for accuracy and completeness?"

His stare said candor or consequences. Failing to come forward in the El Camino hijack attempt was a risk, but trusting the law to do the right thing was a bigger one. I packed the recorder and my notes into my portfolio.

"Since you'll be interviewing my sources, I assume you won't need me any more."

Enright's face hardened into the look policemen got when you didn't take their authority as personally as they did. It told me the interview wasn't over until he said it was over.

"Mr. Spain, this department has zero tolerance for obstruction of justice."

"I'm not obstructing anything. I came in on my own to tell you what I'd learned."

"I'm going to have your statement typed for signature. You are to wait here. I suggest you spend the time giving serious consideration to your future. This investigation will find the truth. However bad it may be, it's better if we hear it from you first."

He had come as close to threatening me as he dared with the video camera running. He collected his portfolio and left me to choke down my terror. In a rare display of good sense, I waited until he was gone before I gave him a succulent raspberry.

His scenario bothered me, and not just because he was casting me as the village idiot. Extortion was a possibility I should have considered. Paige Lomax had made herself an easy target for Sigrid's old acquaintances. Peter Lomax had even suggested as much. I had only an impression Ramona and Skidmore hadn't been in cahoots. If they were up to something it wouldn't make Sigrid's crimes any less real, but it might explain why they had told me less than the whole truth.

Enright opened the door and startled me out of my thoughts. I had expected him to be gone for a while; calling the records department and other agencies to hunt up old case files, scouring my statement for non-conforming facts and generally seeing how little he could make of what I had brought him.

"There has been a change of plans, Mr. Spain. You can leave now. We'll be in touch later."

I stood up in a hurry. I made it a point never to argue with pleasant surprises. They might get the idea they weren't welcome.

Enright blocked the door.

"You are not to discuss what has been said here with anyone."

"The Lomax family has a right to know."

"Just don't answer any questions from the news media."

The *Tilt* buzzer went off in my head. "Why would the news media ask me anything?"

"Benjamin Neiborsky has retained counsel. He turned himself in to the Prosecuting Attorney's office."

Enright was giving me the bum's rush for a reason. L.A.'s finest had been caught flat-footed by Neiborsky's confession. A signed statement about Neiborsky's activities from a sleazy skip tracer who was already under suspicion in another homicide wouldn't look good in the official files. Someone might think the police should have pursued me and my line of inquiry more aggressively and learned the truth on their own.

I left without telling Enright that Neiborsky had shot me. I didn't like the idea he might find out second hand, but it wasn't the sort of thing I could slip into conversation along with a quick goodbye. And I had other things to worry about.

Neiborsky had been several sheets to the wind when he had confessed. I had expected him to sober up and dare the police or anyone else to prove it wasn't fermented hops doing the talking. Instead he found a lawyer. Now the two of them were down at the Prosecutor's office spinning who knew what mix of truth and fantasy to try for the best possible plea bargain.

Part of the fantasy almost certainly included the underhanded methods used by one Henry Spain to extract the confession. The Prosecutor wouldn't be happy. Charging Franklin Winter with felony murder would be a serious political risk. A military officer who had faced a Chinese field army in the mountains of Korea wasn't likely to back down from a county official. The old General was rich enough to put up a very nasty court fight. And the evidence tying him to the woman who did the shooting was flimsy at best.

If there was a photograph that placed Winter at The Shadows with Sigrid Helstrom on New Year's Eve 1944, I needed to find it before I was called on the carpet. I reached Roy Lee on the cell phone. She reminded me lunch was my treat.

Chapter 21

Roy Lee was already seated when I reached her choice of restaurant. The maitre'd had given her a window table with an ocean view. She was money in the bank. She had the class to bring the big spenders out of the woodwork and a smile that let them know only the finest had any hope of being adequate.

She gave me the abridged version when I sat across from her. "You really should do something about your wardrobe, Mr. Spain. You were at your best dressed for a funeral."

I didn't argue. Even on days when I wore a tie, I seldom risked anything beyond basic business attire. I knew there was a line between fashion statement and flood victim, but I had no idea where it was.

"Out of it and proud of it," I quipped.

A frosty look informed me she preferred suave members of the opposite sex. It was just as well. I had already wound up in no end of trouble playing Galahad for a blonde and then made a fool of myself with a client's wife. The last thing I needed was more temptation. I glanced at a manila envelope lying beside her napkin.

"New Year's Eve, 1944?"

"Help yourself."

The Shadows had sounded like a dingy cellar from black and white Hollywood. The background in the age-stiffened 8 X 10 glossies showed an extravagant layout edged in streamlined curves. The band shell accommodated a dozen musicians in tuxedos and a willowy singer in an evening gown. The dance floor was packed and the surrounding tables were crowded. New Year's regalia hung everywhere. Only the number of military uniforms gave any hint that the largest armies ever raised were locked in final combat on the distant battlefields of Europe and Asia.

"How big was this place?" I asked.

"I understand the capacity was around two hundred. The building had its own block along Sunset, just outside what was then the L.A. city limits."

"It looks pretty fancy."

"Ostentatious," Roy Lee corrected. "Even by the standards of the 1940s."

An overdressed waiter arrived with a basket of bread and hit the highlights of the wine list in a condescending patter. Roy Lee knew what she wanted for lunch without looking at the menu. I ordered something called Hong Kong Rice, mainly because it sounded like it didn't require using a knife and fork at the same time.

There wasn't room on the intimate little table to arrange the photos so I had to study them individually. Only one included Sigrid Helstrom. Included wasn't the right word. She dominated the shot. Taller even than some of the men at the table, she wore an upswept hairdo that emphasized her height and a deeply cut neckline that did the same for other assets. The camera had caught the man next to her sneaking a cleavage check.

"Who is the army officer on Sigrid's left?"

Roy Lee turned the photo and studied him. "Probably a studio executive. Those are signal corps insignia on his lapels, and he's wearing oak leaves on his epaulets. Most of the actors and directors were commissioned as Lieutenants and Captains."

"You mean these were just movie people who changed clothes for the duration?"

"The military commissions were real," she said. "The Signal Corps controlled a significant amount of wartime film production. There are miles of celluloid of matinee idols telling recruits how important it was to brush their teeth, and showing them exactly how to go about it."

I went back to the photos. Most of the officers ran to a pattern—well fed and middle aged. The odd man out was a trim lieutenant who might or might not have been a young Franklin Winter. His lapel insignia were the crossed rifles of the Infantry. Ramona Benitez was at the same table. A big smile and strapless dress that was ready to head south of the border gave her a look of being number two and trying harder. I wondered if there was a reason for that.

"Is Malcolm Trevor in any of these?"

"This is Trevor."

Roy Lee used a nicely filed fingernail to slit his throat in effigy. Small and delicate, he sat erect at a table in a back corner and didn't join in the laughter around him. Through the lenses of rimless spectacles intensity was a visible presence in his eyes. It gave me the creeps.

The waiter arrived with lunch. We ate awhile in silence. I had a hard time keeping my mind on the meal. The pictures kept drawing me back.

"How did Sigrid and Ramona rate invitations to New Year's Eve at The Shadows? Those had to be two hundred of the hottest tickets in town."

"If your father couldn't explain that to you, I don't think I can."

"What I mean is how did they score? Why not any other two wannabes?"

"Why not them?"

"For the same party?"

"They roomed together," she reminded me. "They probably moved in the same circle."

"That doesn't explain how Trevor got in."

"You're not that innocent."

I shook my head. "Trevor was a voyeur. Nothing more."

"Trevor was a cipher. You have only a love struck ingenue's view of him."

"I have your view."

"Excuse me?"

"You said Trevor was small time. If the big egos kept him off the credits, why let him into The Shadows?"

"Does it really matter?"

"It's too much coincidence," I said. "Three of the players in our little melodrama, Sigrid, Ramona and Trevor, photographed in the same room on the night in question."

Roy Lee set her silver down and patted her lips with a napkin. "All right, Mr. Spain, you've got something on that conniving, cynical mind of yours."

"Extortion."

"Excuse me?" Icicles hung from the words.

"That's what this has been about from day one. Sigrid, Ramona, Trevor, and Skidmore, in it up to their ears."

"In what, Mr. Spain?"

"Sigrid wasn't a random victim. She was gang raped when a badger game went wrong."

"Oh, please." Roy Lee let her gaze wander out across the vast expanse of the Pacific.

"Imagine you're Sigrid Helstrom. You're a face in the crowd trying to break into movies."

"I'm not Helstrom. I'm not trying to break into movies. And getting a studio executive into bed for blackmail purposes wouldn't have advanced her career. Hollywood was full of lawyers who specialized in getting film industry management out of that kind of trouble."

"The lawyers couldn't have specialized if the trouble didn't exist."

"There is nothing in those photographs to suggest Helstrom was up to anything more sinister than advertising her scenic attractions."

Roy Lee picked up her silver and resumed her meal.

"The pictures themselves suggest it," I said. "Helstrom had to prove she was in the company of her mark. If she had her own photographer take pictures, it would look like a setup. But if the two of them just happened to pop up in a concessionaire's photo, that would be a lot tougher for a studio shyster to argue away."

"No court would waste its time on a hysterical movie hopeful waving a nightclub 8 by 10."

"Sigrid had witnesses. Malcolm Trevor, who knew the movie brass and probably set up the date. Her roommate Ramona, who was present at the Club. Gabriel Skidmore, who took the pictures."

"If you will turn the prints over, Mr. Spain, you will see the concessionaire's date stamp on the reverse. Faded but undeniable."

"Not these pictures. The ones to back up the badger game. The people working the game couldn't rely on a concessionaire to catch Sigrid slow dancing with the mark. They had to have their own photographer inside The Shadows."

Roy Lee dismissed my reasoning with a hopeless sigh. "Skidmore was African-American, so the club wouldn't admit him in the first place. He hadn't paid for a concession, so they wouldn't let him in with a camera. And if they caught him snapping photos of their customers, they'd have thrown him out on his neck."

"Look at the men in the pictures," I ordered.

"In addition to which," she said, pointedly ignoring my instructions, "if Skidmore took the photographs, you would defeat your own requirement for an independent concessionaire, would you not?"

"What do you see?"

"What am I supposed to see?"

"Uniforms. Skidmore had the ultimate concession. He was a photographer with the Army Public Information Office. He could take his camera anywhere servicemen gathered. The studio brass at The Shadows would have been delighted to crack a big smile for the war effort."

Roy Lee danced her fingernails on the tablecloth. "I brought you the pictures like a good little girl. Now I'm entitled to know what you've learned."

I hadn't really learned anything. Enright's harping on extortion had started me thinking. That alone demanded that I bounce it off someone who was playing with a full deck.

"*Folsom Prison Breakout* was Sigrid's first film. If it was released in 1946, when would casting have been done?"

"Probably 1945, depending on how long between shooting and release."

"Ramona's first film was something called *Last Days of Juarez.* Any idea when that would have been cast?"

"What are you driving at?"

"According to Ramona, the men who raped Sigrid were Army officers. One of the officers was Franklin Winter, but there is no reason to suppose the other four were not studio executives in uniform for the duration. Once they got off gingivitis patrol they would be in a position to trade film roles for silence, to inflate Trevor's compensation, to hire Skidmore for a job no other Negro could touch."

She gave me a withering look. "Which tabloid are you schlepping for?"

"That's another thing. *Confidential* magazine wouldn't have been interested in Trevor alone. What they learned was that he had run a badger game on someone with a name that would sell copy."

"Speculation," she said in her coldest Cape Cod drawl.

She was right, of course. And I needed her help to find out how good a guess it was. I fortified myself with a forkful of Hong Kong rice.

"You're a professional researcher, Roy Lee. You know the rules. Run every possibility out to the end and don't turn up your nose at anything."

That got me another look. "You're the clumsiest left handed eater I've ever seen."

"Thanks for noticing."

"It's impossible to miss."

Something flickered in her eyes, but I was probably kidding myself if I thought it was sympathy.

"Can you find out which studio executives who held Army commissions were at The Shadows that night?"

"Judging from the photographs, there were quite a number. How will you know which one fits your theory?"

"Another clue is when the careers of Sigrid and Ramona ended. Were they simultaneous? If so, did that coincide with an event in the lives of one of the executives at The Shadows?"

"What do you really expect to find?"

"Another piece of the jigsaw puzzle. Maybe one with enough design and color so I can see where it fits. Can I keep the pictures awhile?"

"No." She gathered them into the envelope. "I have a class to teach." She stood with effortless grace and a pitying smile. "Tip generously. I do sometimes eat here with eligible men. I'd like the staff to remember me fondly."

Most of the male eyes in the room watched her leave, mine included.

I took my time finishing lunch, partly because of my arm and partly because I was in no hurry to tackle the next item on my agenda. Getting shot again would probably be less painful than telling Paige Lomax that I had just taken her family's secrets public. Or persuading her to tell me whether she had tried to hijack a load of pirate software.

CHAPTER 22

Berkut and Schroeder's PBX operator directed me to the Convention Center, where placards welcomed me to a conference on meeting the challenges of modern parenting. Paige was chairing a panel on protecting children in cyberspace. All the chairs in the room were taken so I slouched against the back wall and listened to the litany of evils that could befall the little darlings if dark forces weren't legislated off the Internet.

Paige wrapped things up and the room started buzzing. Half an acre of women packed shoulder bags and trendy little backpacks for the pilgrimage to the next gathering. Paige made her way through the departing throng to where I stood. Fragrance as dry as the Mojave Desert enveloped me. She kept her voice low, but acid etched every word clearly.

"An admitted felon surrendered himself to the Los Angeles County Prosecutor this morning and implicated my mother-in-law in four homicides. I want an explanation."

"The explanation is simple. Your mother-in-law was responsible for the homicides. I've told you about three of them. If we can find someplace private, I'll fill you in on the fourth."

"This man Neiborsky remained silent for decades. Why did he come forward now?"

"His past was catching up with him."

"Did you panic him?"

"I interviewed him to learn what he knew."

A look that started out condemning me to the lowest level of Hades morphed into a million candlepower worth of charisma. It wasn't for my benefit. A hefty matron had arrived. I was the wrong gender even to be noticed, let alone participate in the conversation. I gathered that the matron headed some sort of committee and was inviting Paige to a meeting at her home in Bel-Air. Paige was full of praise for the matron's good work while she made a note of the engagement. The matron waddled off happy. Paige's smile vanished with her electronic scheduler.

"You should have told me you planned to interview a potentially damaging witness. You should have briefed me on the subject matter and let me make the decision."

"Mrs. Lomax, if I found him, other investigators would have found him. He would have been arrested in full view of every television camera your political opponents could bring to bear."

"My opponents have toadies in the Prosecutor's office. Thanks to your incompetence, they are now positioned to present me with a public relations nightmare at any time during my campaign."

"Face them down or forget your political ambitions," I said. "Those are the only options you ever really had."

Her eyes conceded the point by hating me for making it. "Do you have any more unpleasant surprises for me?"

"That depends on whether you organized an attempt to hijack a truckload of pirate software from El Camino."

The indignation that flared in her eyes looked like the prelude to a tongue lashing, but her lawyer's self-control got the better of it.

"Certainly not," she said in a level voice that wasn't about to be baited by any juvenile trickery.

"Does your pro bono parole client—Victor Bradley, is that his name?—does he live at the Camelot work release facility?"

"Have you been spying on Victor?"

"Someone followed me when I left my last two appointments with you. If you recall, I promised to find out who it was."

"Not Victor. He was with me after you left my office."

"The man's name is Davey." I gave her a description and received only a disgusted look for my trouble. "I got behind him and followed him to Camelot."

"The facility has more than a hundred residents. It's shamefully overcrowded."

"Let's forget social engineering for a minute." I told her about the hijack attempt. "Is El Camino pirating software from the firm where your husband works?"

"Another law firm is handling the matter. It wouldn't be ethical for me to use a spousal relationship to interpose myself."

"And it wouldn't be smart for me to rely on your lawyer-client privilege if you conspired in a felony."

Tiny muscles tensed around her mouth. "That borders on slander, Mr. Spain."

"My only contact with software piracy is a lecture I got from your husband on the subject. Unless someone got the wrong impression about why I was hired and wanted to check me out to see if I posed any threat to them, I don't see any reason for the hijackers to follow me."

"That's not impossible," she said with sudden inspiration. "I'll pass the information on to Peter."

The idea was important enough to write herself an electronic note. Even if she didn't believe it, the theory might earn her a spot on Prescott's legal team without compromising her ethics.

"There's a problem with that," I said, and told her the hijackers' GMC was likely the truck used in an attempt to kill Stevie and me on our way to see Sturtevant.

"I understood," she said tartly, "that the investigation of my mother-in-law's background would have your full attention."

"That was the whole point of the investigation, wasn't it, Mrs. Lomax? You knew there was trouble in your mother-in-law's background. Perhaps from her papers, or something she confided before she died. You wanted to know how much could be found by someone starting from scratch. And you wanted that information to come to you, not Stephanie St. John."

Paige was jostled from behind before she could bite my head off. The room was filling for the next session. We made our way out through an incoming display of defective car seats, collapsing cribs and flammable sleepwear. Eyewitness News was setting up a camera. Paige didn't say anything, but I could see in her face that she didn't like someone else's session getting all the press.

"Well, Mrs. Lomax, did I find it? Or is your secret still out there waiting to be discovered? I ask because what I have found so far doesn't quite make sense."

Pressing a sensitive subject in a hallway full of milling women wasn't to her liking. "This interview is at an end, Mr. Spain. As is your engagement."

"Maybe I didn't make myself clear, Mrs. Lomax. Someone tried to kill me. I don't mind being used. I offer myself for hire, so I have expect a reasonable amount of that. But attempted murder is not reasonable."

"If you had limited yourself to one engagement, and pursued that with the diligence and responsibility I had hoped for, none of this would have occurred."

"All of it would have happened, Mrs. Lomax. It's all connected. A medical student named Eladio Aguilar died in East L.A. because someone tried to kill Alex Sturtevant. The only people with motive to kill Sturtevant are people involved in a conspiracy he is investigating, and the primary source of that motivation is a murder committed by your late mother-in-law."

She tried to silence me with a glare. It didn't work.

"The Spanish language media will keep the pressure on until Aguilar's killer is found," I warned.

"Aside from being another excellent reason to discharge you, I don't believe that affects me."

I could tell she was determined to build a firewall between herself and the problems that were closing in on her, and wasn't interested in anything I had to say.

"I'll prepare a final report, and a statement of your account."

"You understand that report will become part of attorney work product, and that everything it contains will be covered by attorney-client privilege."

"I'm counting on it, Mrs. Lomax."

"When you are ready, I will review your work."

She made it sound like I would never eat lunch in this town again. I left her to convince the mothers of L.A. that she was the concerned parent best suited to lead the city and drove to my office. She hadn't been interested in the details of Cynthia's fourth homicide, which meant she already knew them. The question was had she known them all along, or called the Prosecutor's office before I arrived and gotten a quick summary of Neiborsky's statement. The answer would cost me a call I didn't want to make.

"Twice in two weeks," Terrence Stafford said with his habitually affability. "This is more like it."

Greed had earned me a quick response to my name on his caller ID. "We'll talk about what you want in a minute," I said. "First I need a favor."

I gave him a thumbnail sketch of the situation.

"Twenty minutes," he said, and hung up.

I spent them thinking about Stafford. He'd had half a century to infiltrate the police and the Prosecutor's office. I had no idea how deeply he'd penetrated, but he was smart, patient and had money to invest in contacts that could keep him out of prison. If I had any hope of finding out what Paige had learned from the Prosecutor's office, he was it.

"Henry Spain Investigations," I said when the phone rang.

"You short changed me on the story," Stafford said.

"How so?" I had told him as little as possible and hoped he wouldn't stumble onto something he could use to squeeze me.

"The Prosecutor is looking at charging General Franklin Winter with felony murder."

"What does that have to do with what I asked you?"

"How much to you know about Winter?"

"I talked to him. Once."

"He comes from old money and he rebuilt the family fortune the old fashioned way; stole it and spat in the face of anyone who accused him. If the Prosecutor files charges his lawyers will stalk everyone on the witness list, looking for anything that smells ripe."

That was a not very roundabout way of telling me I had put him and his plans at risk of exposure. I didn't know what I could do about it at this late date, except learn what I'd gotten into so I could figure a way out.

"Paige Lomax?" I asked.

"The cell number you gave me didn't go through the Prosecutor's PBX, so any call she made was probably cell to cell. Doubtful she got any details of Neiborsky's statement. The Prosecutor knows a hot potato when he sees one. The outlines of the statement spread like wild fire, but there's a tight lid on the actual contents."

Which meant Paige Lomax had already known them.

"Thanks," I said. "Expect something lucrative in the mail."

"I don't suppose there's any point in telling you to stay out of trouble?"

"Believe it or not, I'm trying to do just that."

He didn't bother to argue, which probably meant he'd already decided how much risk he was ready to assume before he sent someone around to cancel our arrangement.

I needed more truth than I had been getting, and I needed it now. I brought up Stevie's file on the computer and called her work number.

Chapter 23

"Did you talk to that General Winter?" Stevie asked in a voice that sounded as impatient as I felt.

"Sturtevant was wrong about the Starliner being met by renegade government agents when it landed in California."

"What difference does that make?"

"Winter couldn't have used his sinister government contacts to arrange your father's death if he didn't have any sinister government contacts."

"Then why did he try to kill Alex Sturtevant?"

"If Winter had the resources to make your father's death look like an aviation accident, why would he send someone after Sturtevant with a primitive handgun?"

"You're supposed to find out why."

"Aviation accidents are investigated by the NTSB. Did you talk to anyone there about your father?"

"They're covering up."

"Who did you talk to? I need a name."

Silence.

"Stevie, if you're serious about finding the truth, I can help. If you're not, don't waste my time."

"George Kicinski," she said in a voice that consigned me to her list of also-rans and hung up.

Mr. Kicinski couldn't see me until tomorrow. Today was shot, and so was I. While I was shutting down the computer, the phone rang. Out of habit, I reached for it with my right hand. Scab ripped loose on my arm. It was a minute before the pain subsided enough for me to say anything.

"Henry Spain investigations."

It was Cassandra Freegate. "Jerry found out I was at your place last night."

"Not from me," I said, and had an idea. Arriving home with my arm draining blood, I hadn't been watching for ratty BMWs. If Davey were watching the house, he could've checked the registration in Cassandra's minivan while she was inside and then called Jerry to see how much trouble he could stir up. Davey was already on my list of people to talk to.

Cassandra left me with some parting advice. "If Jerry comes around, let him blow off steam. Reasoning won't help. He just needs to vent."

I slept fitfully that night, dreaming of angry husbands and giant airplanes and bright little interrogation rooms that smelled of the people who had sweated there before me. Through it all Sigrid Helstrom sat naked under an arching madrona tree and laughed at me from beyond the grave.

Draconian security at the Federal building made me late for next morning's appointment with Senior NTSB Investigator George Kicinski.

Kicinski was a compact man in his fifties. A graying goatee at the point of his narrow chin emphasized the somber, intelligent look of his face. We shook hands and I followed him to a small office crammed with shelves of technical manuals. We sat facing each other across a Government Issue metal desk. A *No Smoking* sign hung prominently on the wall. Kicinski put an empty pipe between yellowed teeth.

"Are you a specialist in aviation accidents, Mr. Spain?"

I shook my head. "My approach to air safety is to spend as much time as possible on the ground."

"What do you hope to accomplish?"

"I'd like some insight into the accident that killed Stephanie St. John's father. She said she talked to you."

A sad smile spread Kicinski's thin lips. He opened a bulging folder on the desk and glanced briefly at the contents; a careful man checking his recollections before he opened his mouth.

"The event is referred to as a propeller over-speed. Do you understand the physics involved in aircraft propulsion?"

"Not even slightly," I admitted.

"The thrust of the engines is transmitted to the air in proportion to the speed and pitch of the propellers. Pitch is the blade angle, which determines how much bite the propeller has. Those two factors are controlled by the pilot. In a multi-engine aircraft, all the propellers have to be closely synchronized. If they get out of balance, one side of the airplane will have more thrust than the other, and it will veer off course."

"Kind of like a car pulling to one side when a brake rotor starts to warp?"

"Same principle," Kicinski said, "but with four engines turning, your vehicle is not slowing. Each turbo-prop is capable of many thousand shaft horsepower. The tips of a spinning propeller can approach supersonic speed. Once you get a hundred ton aircraft moving with that kind of force, it's not easy to get it stopped."

I had a gnawing feeling of inevitability. "What exactly happened?"

Kicinski consulted the file. "The aircraft had just completed its landing rollout and was turning onto a taxiway when propeller over-speed occurred on the number four engine." He glanced up and saw I wasn't getting the picture. "Number four is an outboard engine. Are you familiar with the concepts of moment arm and torque?"

I shook my head hopelessly.

"In simple terms it's leverage. The wing is the lever arm. The outboard engines have more leverage by virtue of being farther along the wing from the fuselage, therefore they can exert more turning force."

I nodded to let him know I understood the principle, if not the technical jargon. He returned to the file.

"Propeller over-speed associated with number four outboard engine generated significant uncommanded turning force. Before the crew could react, the aircraft collided with a maintenance building abutting the taxiway. The collision severed a fuel line, spraying Jet B onto hot engine parts. A simultaneous rupture in the nearest fuel tank spread the resulting fire immediately. It happened so quickly that none of the crew was able to evacuate."

There was a photograph in the folder. Even glancing at it upside down I could see how bad things had been. Only the tail section remained. The rest was ashes and fragments lying a rough cross where the airplane should have been. Bits of fire-fighting foam lingered. Judging from the scale of a partially gutted building in one corner, the plane had been huge. It was hard to imagine it vaporizing that completely.

"Is propeller over-speed a common accident?"

"It was one of a series of similar mishaps involving that particular model of aircraft."

"Is there any chance the investigating team could have come to a hasty conclusion when they saw something that looked familiar?"

He took the pipe out of his mouth and shook his head deliberately. "Recurring events have the greatest potential impact on air safety. If anything, we go over them more carefully."

"How do you go over something that has burned to cinders?"

"In this case the accident happened in view of knowledgeable witnesses; several pilots and aircraft mechanics saw it. Everyone agreed on what happened. There was no black box, but forensic experts can reconstruct accurately from residue position, burn patterns and external impact clues."

"All your experts agreed?"

"It wasn't just NTSB investigators, Mr. Spain. The accident burned out a hangar, so we had property insurance adjusters and fire investigators looking over our shoulder. Also, the manufacturer was facing a hefty settlement to the families of the dead crew. Their engineers took our findings apart fact by fact, looking for any way out. They couldn't find one."

I cleared my throat nervously. "I don't mean to be melodramatic, but the question of sabotage has come up."

"It always comes up, Mr. Spain. Tampering with an aircraft is a Federal offense. Even an indication that willful neglect of maintenance might have occurred triggers mandatory involvement by the FBI."

"Were there any indications?"

He shook his head.

"Did you tell Stephanie St. John that?"

"Yes. I did."

"Her reaction?"

"She came in with her mind made up. She went out the same way. Perhaps she showed you a book?"

Shoved it into my face was more like it. "Maybe I can talk her out of the idea. Some other facets of the author's conspiracy theory aren't panning out either."

Kicinski handed me a card. "If you do come across something that suggests we screwed up, give me a call. We're prepared to re-open any investigation any time on competent evidence."

I thanked him and left.

Kicinski hadn't struck me as the type who would drop the ball or sell out, even if he hadn't worked for a straight arrow organization like the NTSB. The number of eyewitnesses, forensic people and hostile experts involved also seemed to rule out honest error.

Either Alex Sturtevant had made up that part of his theory or he had evidence nobody else had seen. It was time to return my borrowed copy of *Blood Money* and find out which.

CHAPTER 24

"So you talked to old man Winter."

Sturtevant's chair creaked as he lowered his bulk onto the cushion. The day had warmed up enough for him to open the trailer windows and thin out the coffee smell. I tossed his copy of *Blood Money* on the desk and helped myself to a seat on the leather couch.

"How much of your story can you prove?"

"Denied the whole thing, did he?"

"I was able to invalidate a key part of your scenario."

"And what part might that be?"

"The Starliner was met by a gang of local criminals. There were no renegade Government agents taking possession of the gold."

Sturtevant let out a booming laugh that probably scared jack-rabbits for a mile. "Spain, you may be a crackerjack investigator in your own field, but you're a neophyte when it comes to the Government. Their guiding principle is plausible deniability. Using criminal gangs as a front is standard practice. Hell, the whole country knows the CIA was going to use the Mob to knock off Castro. That's been testified to in Congress."

"Save the sly winking for the conspiracy buffs. I found one of the gang. He spent yesterday telling his story to the L.A. County Prosecutor."

Sturtevant's eyes lit up briefly, and then got cagey. "What else did you shake out of the old General?"

"He tried too hard to convince me that moving the gold was his idea."

"Harold Lomax didn't have the initiative," Sturtevant declared.

"In the book you portrayed Lomax as weak."

"The badge, the gun, the FBI authority; they were all props to hold up a man who lacked the moral center and personal courage to stand on his own."

"Is that why you thought you could bully him into telling you what he knew."

"What the hell are you talking about?" Sturtevant eyed me suspiciously, a warning that I could hide nothing from the great bearded prophet.

"You sicced Stephanie on him to spy for you. She told you he was going to a charity dinner. You confronted him afterward. Demanded he tell you everything. He was old, confused, frightened. He tried to get away from you. But he got turned around and ran out into the street where he was run down by a drunk driver."

"Horse shit."

"Come on, Sturtevant. A man in his eighties, running out into traffic on his own? You can't expect anyone to believe that."

"What are you trying to pull?"

"You wrote a book demeaning Harold Lomax. You've been harassing General Winter. With that kind of influence behind me, I think I can talk the Prosecutor into involuntary manslaughter."

Sturtevant was the type who turned belligerent when he got scared. Blood rose in his face. Ragged breathing flared his nostrils.

"Don't have a coronary," I said before he could blow up at me. "I don't really think you killed Harold Lomax. I'm just trying to show you how easy it is to wind up on the wrong end of some crackpot's conspiracy theory."

He subsided from belligerent to indignant. "Harold Lomax's death was a major blow to my investigation."

"How much actual evidence have you found?"

Triumph infiltrated his features. "Not much of a poker player, are you, Spain?"

I stared at him, drumming my fingers on the sofa arm.

"You turned your hole card face up," he said. "I can file a Freedom of Information Act request at the Prosecutor's office and get a copy of your witness' statement."

"Gee whiz. Does that mean I won't be mentioned in the acknowledgements of your best seller?"

His eyes narrowed. "If you want anything from me, you'll have to up the ante."

"You don't have anything, Sturtevant. Your ridiculous book died on the shelves, so you came to California looking for evidence to back up the guesswork it was based on. You didn't find any because a lot of your guesses were wrong."

"You don't believe that," he insisted. "You didn't drive all the way out here just to return a book."

"You conned Stephanie into cozying up to Harold Lomax to see what she could learn about her father's death. But there was nothing to learn. It was an accident. You sent me to do the interview you could never get with your criminal mastermind, General Winter. Except Winter isn't a criminal mastermind. He's a tired old man who spent his life being blown by the gales of chance. That's my report to Stephanie, unless you can show me something else."

Sturtevant's poker game wasn't going the way he'd hoped. He unlocked a desk drawer and pulled out a tattered manila folder. Opening it on the desk, he went through the papers inside until he found what he wanted.

"The original is locked in a safe place," he warned, in case I had any ideas.

What he held out was the twenty year old civil complaint of a Tran Thien. Just before Saigon fell, Tran had entrusted a quantity of gold to Brigadier General Franklin Winter for transport to a precious metals firm in Arizona for ultimate sale. When Tran finally got his family to the U.S., he received less money than he expected. I returned the paperwork.

"Was it Tran who contacted Winter? Or Winter who contacted Tran?"

Sturtevant put the affidavit back in the folder and locked the folder away. "It doesn't matter who starts corruption, Spain. Anyone who participates is equally guilty."

"It's a loose end, Sturtevant. Your book is full of them."

"Any book is necessarily a summary. There just isn't room for—."

His face froze. His eyes shifted to an open window.

"What is it?" I asked.

"There's someone out there."

I hadn't heard anything, but this wasn't my turf. "Call the police."

"And wait a week for them to show up?"

He brought his bulk out of the chair and lumbered to the door with his best effort at stealth. The trailer vibrated under his step. He retrieved the combination rifle and shotgun from its perch by the hinges, checked the load and then opened the door. Instead of going through quickly and getting to cover, he stood in the opening peering left and right. If anyone had actually been waiting for him, he would have been impossible to miss.

"Cover my backside," he ordered.

He clumped down the stairs and set off. In his buckskin shirt and moccasins he looked like an overweight and slightly arthritic outtake from *Last of the Mohicans*. I was tempted to use his absence to prowl his desk, but the possibility someone actually had tried to kill him in East L.A. chased me out of the trailer so I couldn't be mouse trapped. I wasn't about to troop off into the badlands following an obvious doofus with a loaded gun.

Sturtevant made his way down from the knoll where the trailer stood and attacked the steep slope behind. Loose stones cascaded down as he struggled upward, half-hidden by stunted foliage that fought for life among the rock outcroppings. He made it to the top and disappeared.

What to make of his behavior I wasn't sure. His conspiracy theories might simply have gotten the better of him. Or he might be staging a little innocent melodrama to keep me interested. Or there might be something sinister behind the show.

The death of Eladio Aguilar had focused more attention on Sturtevant and his book than he'd seen in the last eight years. I couldn't imagine how he might have engineered the killing, but the motivation was definitely there.

I heard him before he actually reappeared, spilling loose rock ahead of him as he fought gravity on the way back down. He arrived at the trailer puffing like an asthmatic teakettle.

"Damned rabbit warren back there. Bastard could've gone up any one of those canyons. Too rocky to cut any sign."

"Come off it, Sturtevant. The only signs you could track by are freeway reflectors."

"You think it's a damned joke, don't you?"

"If somebody wanted you dead, you'd be dead. You were an easy mark going through that door."

He clumped back into the trailer and replaced the gun. Dust and sweat mixed into brown rivulets that ran down into his beard. He sank back into his chair. I sat on the sofa.

"Why would someone pass up umpteen chances to kill you quietly out here, and then make a try for you in Boyle Heights? There are more potential witnesses per square mile in East L.A. than anyplace else in California."

"It's Stephanie. That's who they really want."

"There is no way the killer mistook Eladio Aguilar for Stephanie."

"They had to get me out of the way so they could kill her. They got the wrong man and had to pull back and wait for another chance."

"Why not just catch up with her when you weren't around?"

"They didn't know where to find her. All they had was her E-mail address. They tried for her once when I arranged to meet her in Boyle Heights, and once more when she arranged to bring you out here. The only times they had a physical location on her."

That was the first of his goofy theories that seemed to fit the facts. I knew from experience that Stevie wasn't easy to find. And two shots had been fired when she was either present or expected.

Sturtevant saw that he had my attention and pressed his advantage. "Face it, Spain. She learned something from Harold Lomax. Something she wasn't supposed to know."

"Then why hasn't she mentioned it?"

"She may not know it's significant."

"You're guessing again, Sturtevant. And you're not very good at it."

"All right. You don't have to believe me. But at least help me get the truth out to protect Stephanie. I know you care about her. I could see it when the two of you came out here."

All the suggestion did was remind me of the mid-life crisis that had got me into this mess. "Give it a rest, Sturtevant. Put your talent to work writing the great American novel. This silly project will never sell."

An exasperated wheeze leaked out of him. "I don't understand you, Spain. Your buddies fought and died in Vietnam. Don't you give a damn about them? Don't you care that these bums made a mockery of their sacrifice?"

"No soldier who fought in Vietnam or anyplace else ever gave a rat's ass what the Generals and the politicians did. They cared about the men they served with. Friendship isn't something you can put on a plane and smuggle out of the country."

"I can do it without your help," he warned. "I've got my trap baited."

Either he really was a goofball, or he was setting me up for more theater.

"Changed my Internet password," he revealed. "They're going to have to steal the new one to do any more eavesdropping."

On that note, I left. The drive back to L.A. gave me time to think about Sturtevant and his intruders. If he wasn't lying and someone had stolen his password, the thief would have to be sophisticated to make use of it. Victor Bradley, with his astronomical IQ and the computer science degree he earned in prison, fit the bill nicely. Bradley was indebted to Paige Lomax for taking his parole case, and it was possible Paige was afraid Stevie had learned Cynthia Lomax had killed a man when she picked up the gold from the Starliner. If it came out that the Lomax fortune was based on homicide, Paige stood to lose a lot more than just an election. Of course, it was also possible Cynthia hadn't done the shooting. I had only Neiborsky's word, and he had plenty of possible reasons to lie. Posthumous revenge against Sigrid Helstrom. A chance to shake down her heirs. Or maybe he had done the shooting himself and needed to put the job off on someone else.

I hadn't been at the landing field to meet the Starliner, but a mental image filled my head anyway. Out in the semi-arid flatland, left over from World War II, just a deserted ribbon of cracked concrete and the foundations of a couple of long vanished buildings. A huge airliner dwarfing a couple of trucks. Approaching from the distance, a jeep carrying a man and a woman.

"Georgia Stream," I told my title attorney when I had him on the cell phone. "Can you check her against the death and marriage records?"

"In the opposite order, I presume."

"All I know is she dropped off the face of the earth a quarter of a century ago."

A long sigh came over the connection. "I may be doing the same myself."

"Donna?"

"She wants to talk."

"Do me a favor. Check on Georgia Stream first."

I had the uneasy feeling his talk with Donna would be a lot worse than mine with Cassandra. And I needed to find Georgia Stream. Aside from Neiborsky, she was the only known living witness to the Starliner landing. Assuming she was still alive.

CHAPTER 25

She was Georgia Harris now. Her skirt and blazer probably had cost more than my office rent for the month. She settled in one of the art deco chairs with an unhurried grace that gave me the distinct impression she was in charge and I was a supplicant in my own business quarters.

"My attorney," she said in a voice quiet enough to compel careful listening, "had a conference with the Prosecutor. She received assurances of confidentiality."

"I haven't spoken to the Prosecutor."

"Then how did you find me, Mr. Spain?"

"You were married and divorced in California. You still live in the State. Any competent skip tracer could locate you in less than an hour." I had held off purposely so I wouldn't bump into the Prosecutor's staff.

"Perhaps I should have asked how you knew to look."

"Confidential," I said to avoid admitting I was the one who forced Benjamin Neiborsky to seek a plea bargain.

"What is your interest?" Direct blue eyes wanted to know where a complete stranger got off poking into a sensitive area of her past.

"According to Neiborsky, your escort displayed some pretty erratic behavior. He challenged five armed people and then put himself in the path of a four engine aircraft. I was hoping you could tell me about him. About why he might have done what he did."

"Youth is a time for mistakes. Andrew's were tragic."

"I'm not trying to judge him. Just understand what sort of person he was."

"Andrew was what used to be called a BMOC...big man on campus. A law student destined for great things."

"The newspapers suggested a romance."

Her meager smile condemned me to life among the terminally naive. "I was twenty-one at the time. My best friend from high school was jetting around the world as flight attendant, doing what she referred to as the snake dance with all sorts of exotic men. I was daddy's good girl, providing an upright example for a sorority full of simmering hormones. Andrew was a mildly interesting break in a very dull routine of eager boys hoping for the impossible and arrogant athletes who couldn't believe I wasn't throwing myself at their feet."

"How did you wind up in the badlands?"

"Sounds ridiculous, doesn't it? A date in the desert."

I didn't say anything.

"In the seventies, the environment was very chic. Particularly among people too young to have a fully developed understanding of how dangerous a place the world could be."

A distant siren reminded me it wasn't just the desert. "How did you wind up at the landing site?"

"We saw the plane coming down. It was huge, but it was going so slowly it just seemed to float. It looked like it landed right over the next rise. We could see the top of it and we caught glimpses of people using a forklift to unload the cargo, but we just kept driving and driving and never seemed to get any closer. They were finished by the time we actually reached the landing field."

"What kind of reception did you get?"

"They didn't pay any attention to us until Andrew got out of the jeep and started yelling at them to stop what they were doing."

"Didn't you say they were finished?"

"They were putting the forklift on their truck. Getting ready to leave."

"Why did Andrew try to stop them?"

"I think he wanted to impress me," she said with a touch of embarrassment. "He didn't actually propose marriage, but he did give me a very detailed description of the life he'd planned for himself and his chosen bride. After two days of it, the sorority full of hormones looked pretty good. I'm sure he sensed that I'd lost interest."

Dynamic law student slays Starliner, rides off into sunset with socially acceptable fair maiden. It was just trite enough to be true.

"Who was in charge at the landing field?"

"A woman."

"Can you describe her?"

"Impatient. Whip-cracking"

"What about physical characteristics?"

"Tall. Nordic. About fifty."

Georgia's short, emotionless answers told me she wasn't comfortable discussing Sigrid Helstrom.

"What about the men?" I asked.

"One of them was very polite. He asked me to calm Andrew down. He said there didn't have to be trouble."

Bunny, the gentleman. "And the others?"

"Just laborers. Two loading the forklift and a third out in front of the plane with a fire extinguisher."

"Was there a problem?"

"They were starting the engines." She shivered at the memory. "The plane was gigantic. The tires were taller than I was. They started the engine closest to us first. This huge propeller began to turn. Then there was an ear-shattering explosion. Fire and black smoke belched out of the exhaust pipe. I think I screamed, but I couldn't hear it over the noise. The exhaust pipe kept burning, like a blowtorch. I hunkered down in the jeep and thought I was going to die. Finally the fire blew itself out and they went on to the next engine."

"What happened when they had them all lit?"

"Andrew lost it. He ran out in front of the plane, waving his arms. I couldn't hear what he was yelling. Two of the men pulled him back when the plane started to move. I closed my eyes against the blowing sand and put my fingers in my ears, but I still heard the shot."

She paused to be sure I grasped the enormity of what she was saying.

"Andrew was lying face down. His ankles were crossed, like a picture of a dead policeman I once saw in the newspaper."

"Did you see who shot him?"

"The woman had a pistol in her hand."

Neiborsky had told the truth.

"What happened then?"

Laser eyes told me to forget about tawdry details. "I wound up in Mexico City, where businessmen needed a blonde gringa as a party favor after they closed a big deal, and where officials had dignitaries to entertain. I had no idea how strong my survival instincts were, how much I could endure to stay alive. I learned Spanish one beating at a time. I made friends with whores who spit on me. I cleaned toilets. I learned more about myself in seven months than I had learned in all the twenty one years before."

"How did you get back home?"

"One night they took me and several other girls to a reception. We were supposed to make the rounds. Put ourselves on display. We'd be bought for private parties afterward. I wound up with a tipsy banker who thought his new Porsche made him a caballero. I told him I wouldn't lay him unless he had the cojones to go horn honking past the U.S. Embassy. When we got there, I shut down Zorro's pretty little ride in the middle of the street, tossed the keys and made a run for it. He was too wobbly to catch me before I got to the gate and not quite drunk enough to get physical with the Marine on duty."

Escaping on her own might have explained how she got home without an investigation turning up a lot of facts on the way to finding her. If it had been true.

"What did the police do when you got back?"

"They asked endless questions. Everything from what happened to Andrew to what kind of drugs were on the plane. My attorney learned that from the Prosecutor it was actually contraband gold. She's afraid I might be called as a corroborating witness if anyone files a civil claim."

"That isn't why I called you, Mrs. Harris. I also had nothing to do with the attempt to hijack your truck."

Her face fell dangerously still. "How much do you really know, Mr. Spain? Please be truthful. It's very important. To both of us."

"You're up to your elegant neck in software piracy," I told her. "The men you met in Mexico City all those years ago are now senior business and political leaders with the power and organization to protect and trans-ship large quantities of full package product. You're cashing in on those contacts."

"I have to be sure you're not just guessing."

"To start with, you need a better fairy tale about your time in Mexico. Beatings are a quick way to keep campesino harlots in line, but high end clients object to bruises. A carefully administered taste of suffocation is a lot cleaner and just as persuasive. And your escape was pure cineplex. Your handlers wouldn't have been that careless."

Her flawless composure conceded nothing. "And what do you think happened?"

"You were bought by business people. You were just money to them. They would have calculated your value as white cargo then contacted your family and quoted a higher figure as ransom. Perhaps you had to earn your keep during negotiations, but eventually you were returned for payment."

"You seem very sure of that, Mr. Spain."

"I'm a skip tracer. Recovering lost children is a large part of my income."

In my days as a national agency hooligan I was the one who spoke gutter Spanish so I was the one who wound up sitting on the hood of a private ambulance at two in the morning at a wetback crossing along the San Ysidro river; a .45 under my coat and a briefcase crammed with cash on my lap; trying to calm a jittery doctor who did no-questions-asked jobs to support his pharmaceutical habits; listening to the scanner on the Border Patrol tac frequencies; hoping the other agency goons would keep their heads down in the bushes and their automatic rifles on safety. There was no reason to think Georgia's exchange had gone any differently.

"How did you connect me with El Camino?" she asked.

"You came alone to see a man you'd never met. That implied you were afraid I knew something you couldn't share even with your lawyer. Then you confided things no woman would confide unless her need for privacy was overridden by something immediate and ominous. Only the hijack attempt I blundered into came remotely close."

"And where else did I blunder?" She sounded more curious than chagrined.

"You were uncomfortable talking about the woman at the landing strip. Somehow you learned who she was, and that her son was an executive at Prescott. You're managing the L.A. operation of El Camino as a way of getting even."

"Necessity, Mr. Spain, not revenge." Sadness touched her voice. "Mr. Harris learned about my past. He never found the courage to call me damaged goods to my face, but he and his considerable income were gone soon enough."

"I stand corrected."

"What are you?" she asked. "You're too smart to be a retired policeman."

"Retired juvenile delinquent."

There was irony in her laugh. "Life has a perverse way of turning us into the last thing we expect to become. Do you know what I was planning to do when I got my sociology degree?"

I shook my head.

"Rehabilitation work. Teach former convicts how to lead normal lives. Now my children are in out-of-state boarding schools. My home has state of the art anti-intrusion. Both the Lexus and the Land Rover are bullet proof. I wouldn't dare drive to Safeway without an automatic pistol under the seat."

"Is it really that bad?"

"I mention it to let you know I can't guarantee my own safety. Certainly not yours."

My blood chilled a few degrees. "Lucky for me I'm not one of the investigators trying to put you out of business."

"Then how did you get involved?"

"It's too long a story to tell, Mrs. Harris. And I couldn't tell it convincingly, because I'm not sure in my own mind which parts are true and which aren't."

Her smile vanished and she stood. "I don't expect to hear from you again, Mr. Spain."

Her exit left the delicate residue of a fragrance I hadn't noticed when we were engrossed in conversation. The scenario behind her visit wasn't hard to reconstruct. El Camino's thugs had reported my license number after the hijack attempt. For all I knew, they used the same pipeline into DMV that I did. My phone directory listing as a private investigator wouldn't have gone down well, and my call to Georgia would have set off alarm bells. She had come, or been sent, to learn what I knew and what I wanted. She probably didn't believe my winding up in the middle of the hijack was an accident any more than I did.

My rear view was getting crowded. In addition to an angry husband, an angrier client, a police homicide investigation and my own past, I now had a gang of Latino cutthroats eyeing me. I also hadn't forgotten the possibility that an unknown killer was stalking Stevie. If I didn't regain the initiative, both of us could wind up dead. I called Peter Lomax for an appointment.

CHAPTER 26

I spent twenty minutes in Prescott's reception area, watching employees return from lunch and click their way through the glass doors with picture ID badges. It was all as pointless as a child's security blanket. The bits and bytes were being stolen as fast as they arrived.

Peter Lomax finally came out in his starched shirt and sport coat to escort me to his office. There was no chit-chat this trip. I opened my portfolio on his conference table.

"As your wife probably told you, she is terminating my engagement."

"Yes, she did tell me."

He settled back in his executive throne and didn't bother to challenge my inference that Paige called all the shots. I put two sheets of computer printout in front of him.

"This is a statement of your account. You are due a nominal refund. If you agree, please sign both copies. One is for your records. You'll have a seven-day recission period. If I haven't heard from you by then, I'll send a check."

"Paige indicated you would be making a final report." He removed his rimless spectacles and began polishing the lenses with an impregnated tissue. It was probably his way of reminding me who was in charge and letting me know my work was in for some serious scrutiny.

"Your wife asked that I telephone her for an appointment," I said, emphasizing again who was giving the orders. "You are welcome to attend, or to receive a separate written copy, if you wish. Since you signed the retainer check for the marital community, I thought I should complete the financial arrangements with you."

"Yes. Of course."

He didn't seem as perturbed as I'd hoped by the obvious suggestion that he existed just to pay the bills. He replaced his spectacles and began reviewing my arithmetic, as if he knew there would be unpleasant consequences if even the slightest mistake turned up later.

"Has El Camino relocated?" I asked.

He smiled at my juvenile attempt to startle him. "Yes, Paige did mention you thought someone might have misunderstood your assignment."

"That was before I talked to Georgia Harris."

He started to say something, but thought better of it and went back to the invoice.

"You can see how it looks," I said.

He set aside the designer pen he was using to tick off numbers and sat back again. "How what looks?"

"A man follows me from your home. Later he follows me from your wife's office. That same evening he's involved in an attempt to hijack a load of pirate software from El Camino."

"What are you suggesting?"

"Your firm's business is being hurt by El Camino's piracy. The local head of El Camino has damaging information about your mother's background. You retained me to investigate and then had me followed as a hunter follows a bird dog, to see what game I'd flush. You had El Camino hijacked both to warn them away from Prescott and to scare Georgia Harris into silence."

He stared like he wasn't sure of my sobriety or my sanity. Either he was the real actor in the family or he didn't know about the connection between his mother and Georgia Harris. I got the definite impression he hadn't sent anyone to hijack El Camino.

"Whose idea was it to hire me, Mr. Lomax? Yours or your wife's?"

"I beg your pardon?"

"Your wife said she took the call when the police phoned to check on whether Stephanie St. John had permission to use your late father's Bentley?"

"Paige happened to be nearer the phone."

"What did she say when she told you about it?"

"Mr. Spain, this matter is no longer your concern." His tone warned me that I was putting his anger management skills to the test.

"One of you decided to hire me to do a background investigation of your mother. I'd like to know who made the decision, and what you thought I'd find."

"I don't see that it matters. You were hired to locate vindictive former acquaintances. Clumsiness aside, you've succeeded. That, I believe, completes your assignment."

"Not quite, Mr. Lomax. There is one outstanding question."

"What might that be?"

"Your mother's film career."

"What about it?"

"Why did it exist?"

"Excuse me?" Sigrid Helstrom and her films had been part of his life from childhood. He had probably never thought to question how they came into being.

"She wasn't critically acclaimed," I pointed out.

"Few film performers are."

"I never heard of a Sigrid Helstrom fan club."

"If you are suggesting promiscuity as…"

"I'm not."

That mollified him only a little.

"You see, Mr. Lomax, the question is this: out of the thousands of ambitious and attractive young women who came to Hollywood, how did your mother score?"

"She was a determined woman. A hard worker."

"She still would have needed an edge."

"A skilled agent, perhaps."

"Skilled agents don't waste time on small commissions."

"Blind chance, then," he said impatiently. "Frankly I don't see any point to this conversation."

"My guess is blackmail, but I think you'd better ask your wife to be sure."

"Paige?"

"She's the attorney for your mother's estate."

"Are you suggesting my wife has withheld something from me?"

"The consequences of your mother's activities didn't die with her. You need to learn what those activities were. Denial is not an option."

"I think I've had just about enough of your cheap insinuations, Spain."

He scribbled a signature on one copy of his statement and thrust it at me. I zipped it into my case and stood.

"Since this was an honest engagement given in good faith and wasn't meant to distract me from any inquiry involving Stephanie St. John, I'm sure you won't mind if I focus my efforts on her now."

Lomax escorted me to the lobby and sent me away without the customary handshake. I left hoping I had rattled him enough to send him tiptoeing to Paige to give a little boy tug on her skirt and ask why that nasty man was saying all those terrible things.

From Lomax's office I drove straight home. Phase two of my plan called for just the right outfit, crackerjack timing and a fair amount of stupidity on my part. I was pretty sure I could muster the stupidity.

A checked shirt and chinos were a nice start toward meeting the wardrobe requirements. A mail order corduroy sport coat removed any possibility that I had taste or style. Worn loafers provided a nice accent of impending bankruptcy. There weren't many looks I could do really well, but I did seem to be able to handle pathetic hustler.

On the way to the Camelot Apartments I checked the tavern lot where Davey had parked the other day. His BMW wasn't there. That didn't prove anything, but it was a promising sign. I parked behind Camelot and settled in to watch the dumpster.

A shamefully overcrowded halfway house had to produce a lot of trash. Sooner or later someone had to bring the trash out. Granted, it wasn't the best idea I'd ever had. The later could turn out to be much later. And this wasn't a neighborhood where I wanted to spend a lot of time sitting alone and exposed in a parked car. But given the protective nature of California Corrections System, knocking on the front door wouldn't get me very far. As long as I was hoping, I decided to hope for someone noticeably smaller than I was, preferably the nervous type.

Disappointment was quick in coming. A hefty black shouldered his way through a door manhandling a garbage can that probably weighed as much as I did. I bailed out of the Volvo and double-timed along the walk hoping this guy wasn't named Ernesto.

"Hey, man," I called before he could disappear inside.

From a distance he had looked big. Close up he was gargantuan. Six feet eight inches from the soles of his purple Nikes to the top of a bullet head. Three hundred pounds of iron muscle bulged inside an XXL Tweety Bird T-shirt. Sweat stained the armpits and poisoned the air around him. His tattoos had two main themes: edged weapons and blunt instruments. Subtle he wasn't.

"Who you?" he asked suspiciously.

I gave him a nervous grin. "Abraham Lincoln. Here's my identification."

He took the five-dollar bill I handed him and turned it over in his thick fingers. A smile formed slowly on his full lips.

"Yeah." His voice was an ominous purr. "Thought I recognized you."

I felt my grin stabilize. "Look man, you know Davey, don't you?"

"I ain't the social type."

I described Davey.

"Specially with no pill poppin' white trash."

"Look, man, Davey told me had some leads for me."

"Say what?"

"You know, dudes that needed a little cash and could make the weekly bee."

He eyed me skeptically. Looking like a two-bit hustler for the loan sharks wouldn't be enough. I had to back it up with some fast talk.

"Only I ain't heard from him," I went on. "He's took up with this dude. Bradley or something. He's got no time for business no more."

Tweety Bird hawked up a throat full of phlegm and launched it in the general direction of the dumpster. I hoped it represented his opinion of Bradley, not me.

"Victor," I said. "That's his name. Victor Bradley. Good lookin' dude. Big brain. Thinks he's God's gift to the planet, you know. Got this parole thing he's working on."

"So?"

"So maybe you could tell Davey I'm still waiting to do business?"

"Rimmer's a disease. I wouldn't want to catch none of it talkin' to him."

Davey's last name was a bonus. I decided to try for more.

"Maybe you know where he's working?"

"You try the Union Hall?"

"What local?"

"I thought you knowed him."

The mammoth black loomed over me. He had a dumpster handy to stash the body. I felt my grin flicker.

"Maybe he told me. I don't remember those details. I just wanted leads off him, you know, man?"

His eyes got cagey. "What name I give him?"

I handed over another five.

He pocketed it and smiled. "Yeah," he purred. "Mistah Fimp."

I thanked him and left. His probation was probably the only thing that had kept him from pulling out my arms and legs to get at whatever stray nickels and dimes I hadn't given him.

My shirt was stuck to my skin when I got into the Volvo. The good news was that Tweety Bird hadn't argued when I linked Davey with Victor Bradley. As bad as my acting had been, Bradley would know within the hour that I had been asking about Davey Rimmer. He would want to know why.

The big question was Paige Lomax. If she wanted Alex Sturtevant and Stevie St. John killed, a parole hearing was a good way to get someone out of prison to do the job. If so, she'd have Peter on one side wanting to know what she was up to and Bradley on the other, pestering her to do something permanent about me. I tried not to dwell on the possibilities.

CHAPTER 27

A manila envelope lay on the carpet just inside my office door. A sticky explained that Marisol had found the enclosed 8 X 10 photographs among Ramona's possessions. Included was a perfumed note in a spidery feminine hand instructing her to forward them to me. I cleared space on the desk and laid them out.

The backgrounds matched those in Roy Lee's photos taken at The Shadows on New Year's Eve, 1944. One caught Malcolm Trevor in a furious argument with the Signal Corps officer who had been inspecting Sigrid Helstrom's cleavage. I found the officer's name on the back. The neat block printing was familiar. I had seen it when I read Gabriel Skidmore's notes on the Caliente Beach Club. I grabbed the phone and pressed out Roy Lee's number.

"Who was Arthur Mazmanian?" I asked as soon as I heard her pick up.

"Studio Vice-President, and hello Mr. Spain, it's nice to hear your voice again, too."

The ice in her Cape Cod drawl was a none too subtle reminder that she was a lady, and would be treated as such, thank you.

I mumbled a lame apology. "Did you recognize him in the picture with Sigrid Helstrom?"

"Not while you and I were looking at it, if that's what has you sounding so grouchy."

"Can you give me some background?"

"Arthur 'The Ape' Mazmanian was charged with keeping order in a studio full of free spirited creative talent. His methods were heavy handed. He tapped phones, opened mail, had people followed and hired thugs to discourage labor unrest. You and he would have gotten on famously."

That was probably just a gratuitous insult. I doubted she knew any of my background.

"Thanks," I said.

"An unsavory reputation does not mean Mazmanian was involved in an assault on Helstrom, if such an assault in fact occurred."

"A Speed Graphic doesn't lie."

"You have a photograph?"

Her disbelief was almost laughter, but the pictures were undeniable. Besides Mazmanian and Trevor arguing, one showed infantry Lieutenant Franklin Winter and three more showed two Captains and a Major, all wearing Signal Corps insignia. Hollywood executives in uniform for the duration, probably hoping to score a few points with old General Winter by taking his son out for a night on the town.

The sixth told the story.

"It's a little grainy," I told Roy Lee, "but the sheet film they used in those days was big enough to catch plenty of detail."

The print was probably an enlargement of part of a negative. A doorframe intruded obliquely in one corner, suggesting a hasty exposure. Beyond the door was an office. Sigrid Helstrom cringed against a desk. The rag she clutched in a not very successful effort to cover herself had probably been her evening gown.

Arthur Mazmanian was tying his necktie while he talked to a big, hard-looking man. I turned the photo over to check the big man's name. He had been the sole fatality when Sigrid took down The Shadows five years later.

"Any rumors about Mazmanian and the Mob?" I asked.

"He was notorious for entertaining hoodlums in his office at the studio." Suspicion infiltrated her drawl. "What exactly does this photograph show?"

I described it.

"Not enough," she said. "The police would have smelled publicity stunt. A lawsuit would have been only a minor annoyance. A few hundred dollars in hush money at most."

"You keep trying to see this in a Hollywood context."

"Hollywood was the context."

"World War II was the context. Mazmanian was in uniform and subject to court martial. And he had involved the son of a General in his shenanigans."

"The payoff didn't happen until after Mazmanian left the service. At least according to your theory."

"Discharge wouldn't absolve him of crimes committed in uniform. Under the law, he could be recalled to active duty for trial and punishment."

The Army had used that to keep troops in line in Vietnam. I assumed it was true for World War II as well.

"Even so," Roy Lee said, "you do have some Hollywood context. If Trevor were running badger games, word would have gotten out. He would have been blacklisted."

"I think this was a one shot deal. And I think it was Sigrid's idea."

"You think?"

"Sex is a woman's weapon."

"Then why was Trevor involved?"

"Ramona told me she and Sigrid used to hit the night spots hoping to hook up with anyone who could get them into a studio. They were striking out because they had no contact with the men they were hoping to seduce. Trevor talked with studio executives on some semi-regular basis. Ramona showed me a photograph of her and Sigrid taken at Big Sur. I think that was Trevor's sales pitch."

"In other words you are guessing."

"Not entirely. We know Trevor was at the Shadows New Years Eve. He didn't have the clout to arrange his own invitation. Mazmanian probably told him to bring the girls and fade into the background."

"Ramona wasn't molested," she reminded me.

"Ramona wasn't Sigrid. If you mix several men all wanting the same woman, too much liquor and some accommodating gangsters, it's easy to see how things could turn out as they did."

"Not see, Mr. Spain. Imagine. The word you want is imagine."

I described the photo of a normally meek Malcolm Trevor arguing with Arthur 'The Ape' Mazmanian.

"And you have it in that oak head of yours that Trevor used the assault on Helstrom to blackmail Arthur Mazmanian into providing careers for the four of them?"

"Trevor already had a career. I think he took his in salary and bonus."

"What did you take yours in? Some powerful hallucinogen, I presume."

"When did Mazmanian leave the studio?"

"In the mid-fifties."

That was a quick answer. "You probably also checked and learned that was when Sigrid left film work."

"I didn't check anything. Television became firmly established in the mid-fifties. Motion picture profits languished. Mazmanian's studio was sold."

"Putting Sigrid and Ramona out of work."

"According to you."

"The timing is right," I said. "And I'll bet it's the right studio."

Her brief silence confirmed my theory. "How did you come by the photographs after all these years? Or do I not want to know?"

"Hell hath no fury like a woman scorned."

In my mind's eye I could see flirty Ramona and serious Sigrid, rooming together in wartime Hollywood and trying to meet anyone remotely connected with a film studio. One of them had stumbled across a frustrated introvert named Malcolm Trevor. Trevor was a gentleman, something neither of them had probably seen much of. They both went after him. Sigrid won and Ramona never forgave her.

"Tabloid stuff," Roy Lee said in a voice that placed me firmly under the same rock.

"The *Confidential* Magazine file on Trevor," I recalled.

"What about it?"

"I think I'm looking at it. Ramona sold these photos to *Confidential*. They bought because the pictures tied a high profile studio executive to a tabloid crime. They weren't chasing Trevor. They were chasing Mazmanian. Studio gossip probably told them Trevor had some sort of hold over him."

"And, of course," Roy Lee said, "they went out of business before they could publish, so your fantasy can never be disproved."

"Between the two of us, we can find out."

"My invoice will be in the mail," she said. "It will be marked 'final' for a reason. Prompt payment will be appreciated."

She hung up and left me alone with my thoughts.

If Ramona had a copy of the photos to sell to *Confidential* and another to send to me, then the other conspirators had copies as well. Trevor had found Skidmore taking stills in connection with military training films and recruited him not only because his uniform gave him entrée wherever the scheme took them, but also because he had access to a military darkroom to print up plenty of insurance.

Paige Lomax would have found Sigrid's among her effects. Now all I needed to learn was whether Paige was ready to commission murder to keep the story quiet. I packed the pictures back in their envelope and locked them in the desk.

It was past four, too late to start anything new, so I closed up to head home. The building garage had been almost full when I got back from Camelot. The only spot I had been able to find was on the windowless bottom level. I got off the elevator to find Davey Rimmer sitting on my Volvo.

CHAPTER 28

"Off the trunk, punk."

Davey hopped down before he realized that the habits of prison had him jumping at any order someone barked. Resentment filled his jittery eyes.

"I been waiting on you, asshole."

I caught an aftertaste of marijuana on his breath. If he had to fortify his nerve, he probably hadn't come of his own choosing.

"Where's Victor?" I asked.

"You hear me, asshole?"

Davey's part of the act was to distract me so I would forget Victor Bradley existed. Bradley saw it wasn't working and emerged from between two parked vans.

The clean-cut young man from Berkut and Schroeder was gone. The polite smile had twisted itself into a sadistic anticipation of unpleasant things to come. Whatever he had in mind hadn't been worth shaving for. His prison gym muscles did their bulging in a collarless knit shirt that hung out over faded jeans. His footwear caught my eye. He had cared enough to steal the very best. Alex Sturtevant had said the tracks around his trailer were made by expensive hiking shoes.

"Victor, I don't think the Department of Corrections is going to approve of your field trips into the badlands."

He edged around behind me until he was just a reflection in a window. "You been putting your ugly face where it don't belong."

Davey shuffled, doing his best to stand his ground. "You been putting your pecker where it don't belong."

In less than a minute I would be trapped between two convicts. But bad as the situation was, I had called this meeting and it might be my only chance to test my theory. No smarter than Davey seemed to be, he looked like a good place to start. I tried to sound cool.

"The police have your number, Sonny. You shouldn't have taken that ratty BMW into East L.A."

The flash of panic in his eyes made me wonder if he actually had been ticketed. "Fucking cops don't know shit," he said, and verified he had at least been there.

Bradley's reflection stopped moving. Maybe he wanted to hear how much I knew. Maybe he just wanted to see how far someone could push Davey. I wondered how tight he and Davey really were.

"The ticket is on your car, Davey. About all you can do is turn state's evidence. Tell them you just drove. Tell them you didn't know Victor was going to shoot anyone."

"Think you're fucking smart, don't you?"

"Your pal Victor did do the shooting, didn't he? He didn't hang out at Camelot and fix himself up with a nice alibi while he sent you to do the dirty work?"

That was too good a guess. Davey jammed one hand into a pocket. I had to put him out of action before Bradley could react. I grabbed his wrist and snapped a kick into his shin. He yelled and dropped to one knee. His hand came out of the pocket wrapped around a metal cylinder about the size of a cigar tube. It flashed through my mind that it was probably the makeshift smoothbore gun he had used on Eladio Aguilar. I immobilized him with an arm bar and hooked a kick into his solar plexus.

That put him on the floor, gagging and holding his midsection. The cylindrical gun rolled idly on the concrete. Even if I could reach it, I wouldn't have time to figure out the mechanism. Bradley had recovered from his surprise. His reflection was closing on mine. Adrenaline made me quick for my age. I actually got an arm up in time to block him.

A fat lot of good that did me.

All I saw was the flash of the electric spark. I didn't know how many thousand volts he had in the stun gun, but it was enough to short-circuit me. One second I was standing, the next I was on my back.

My only sensation was looking up at the world from the bottom. Standing over me, Bradley was at least nine feet tall. Davey came unsteadily into my range of vision and stood over me. It looked like he was kicking me. I couldn't feel anything, but all the moves were there.

Bradley wasn't amused.

"Quit fucking around. Get the car."

We had all been transported into a huge metal drum. Bradley's voice was still echoing when Davey spoke in the same hollow reverberation.

"I'm gonna do this fucker right here."

"That ain't the plan," Bradley said.

"Oh, yeah. The plan. The big fucking plan. Who gives a shit where this fucker gets it?"

"Him and Sturtevant are going to get whacked by home invaders," Bradley insisted. "That's the only way this deal works."

"So that bitch lawyer can get on the fucking City Council?"

"That's power, Man. That's juice."

"It's fucking a waste. She don't even know you're pulling this crap to get her elected."

"And she won't know until it's too fucking late."

"Late for what?" Davey wanted to know.

"Once she's on the Council, she can't say shit. She can't prove she didn't know what we did. She does what I tell her or I turn her in to the cops. We own her."

"Yeah. Right. And we're gonna get cash and a couple cars for a bonus."

"Hey, I talked to the dude. He's pissed about Spain and his old lady. He'll come through."

"Like your big contacts from the cell block come through hijacking that truck? Man, what a hand job. You and your big fucking plans. Grab all that stupid fucking software. Sell it for millions. Big fucking bust."

"I gave you a simple fucking job to do in East L.A.," Bradley shot back. "You couldn't even handle that."

"I didn't see you out there giving me no help. You and that big computer brain. All you told me was whack some dude in a cream-colored station wagon. Big brain. Big contacts. Big nothing."

Bradley gave Davey a shove. He was two inches taller and a lot huskier. Davey stumbled back three steps before he could stop. Bradley got in his face.

"You wanna argue with me?"

"Be cool, Man. I just…"

Bradley shoved him back another three steps and got in his face again.

"You wanna argue with me?"

"No, Man."

"Then get the fucking car."

Davey took a couple of limping steps, stooped painfully and retrieved the single shot metal cylinder from the floor. He pointed it in the general direction of Bradley and me. I didn't know which of us he was pointing it at. Bradley didn't seem to care. Davey gave it up and limped off.

Bradley went through my pockets, took my garage access card and replaced my wallet. My car keys were the only other things that interested him. Then everything around me began to move in a slow vertical circle. The floor became the wall and cars clung there in defiance of gravity. I realized Bradley had rolled me onto my side. Enough feeling had returned that I knew when he fastened my hands behind my back with steel cuffs.

The dirty tires of Davey's BMW rolled past my head. He stopped with the engine running and exhaust blowing into my face. Bradley opened the trunk and took out a shoulder weapon; a twin of the combination rifle/shotgun standing on its butt plate in Alex Sturtevant's trailer. Probably the gun I had seen being pulled into the cab of the GMC after Stevie and I were shot at. Bradley unlocked the driver's door of my Volvo, put the weapon inside then opened my trunk. He and Davey picked me up by the feet and shoulders. I was a spectator to what was developing into my execution. I decided it was time to put up a fight. Unfortunately there was a chasm of nonexistent motor coordination between deciding and actually doing. All I could manage were a couple of spasmodic twitches.

Bradley gave me a booster shot. After that the battle consisted entirely of them slinging my limp carcass into the trunk of the Volvo. I didn't bend in enough places to fit well, but they weren't particular. They jammed me in the best way they could and slammed down the lid. The darkness was total.

Bradley's voice came low and muffled. "Get down to the law office. Use that key I made and phone from there, so it shows up right on the caller ID at Camelot. Tell them I'm getting ready for a hearing and I'll be late. Tell them I'll bring a note on the Attorney's letterhead."

"That ain't gonna fucking fool nobody."

"I got copies of the letters the bitch did the other times. They're all the same. I can do her signature better than she can."

"You sure that voice box is going to make me sound like a fucking broad?"

"Just don't fuck up the call. Read it exactly like I wrote it down and hang up."

A car door slammed. The BMW snarled away. The following silence was as empty as a freshly dug grave. I filled it with thoughts of my own stupidity.

It had never occurred to me that Bradley might try to make a pawn of Paige Lomax. Sturtevant and I were a couple of murders not just to clear her way onto the city council, but to hold over her head once she was there. He probably had stalked Sturtevant to East L.A. to put the crime in city jurisdiction. When Davey blew it, he had to take what opportunity offered him. First an attempt to kill Stevie and me on the way to Sturtevant's and now Sturtevant and I were going to fall victim to nonexistent home invaders.

Looking back on Bradley's botched schemes, it was easy to see him as too smart for his own good; his astronomical IQ generating over-complicated, impractical ideas. But he wasn't the one who was handcuffed in the trunk of his own car. And I certainly wouldn't be telling the police about his plans while they zipped me into a body bag out in Sturtevant's trailer.

The Volvo bounced. The door closed. I imagined Bradley getting himself situated in the unfamiliar driver's seat. I wondered how long it had been since he had driven any car. There wouldn't be much call for it in prison.

Bradley validated my worst fears. He started the engine and then killed it trying to back out of the stall. Two more starts and a squeak of tires got us clear. I knew that because I heard him grind the transmission into first and felt the tentative lurch of forward motion. I didn't know what to expect when he got us into L.A. rush hour traffic. It would be just my luck to be killed in a freeway crash on the way to my own murder.

CHAPTER 29

The effects of the stun gun faded. My arm burned where the electrical contacts had arced through my coat and shirt sleeves. My ribs hurt where Davey had kicked me. Exhaust fumes made my head ache. We didn't seem to be making much progress, so I was probably inhaling gridlock.

Not that I was in any hurry. As soon as we got out to Sturtevant's, Bradley would indulge his homicidal urges, let off a little more steam ransacking the trailer to fake a rural home invasion and take off in Sturtevant's jeep, as if the perpetrators had headed for the deep weeds. Any chop shop would make short work of the vehicle.

The police would do likewise with Bradley's cover-up. Two subjects in a homicide investigation dead by violence would set off enough alarm bells to wake even the L.A. cops. Burglary Auto Division would find the chop shop and ID Bradley. Enright would link him to Paige Lomax and break his alibi. None of which would do the late Henry Spain any good. I rolled myself into a ball to see if I could work the cuffs under my feet and get my hands in front of me.

The chain hung up on one heel. I tugged. The loafer flew off and rattled against the wall of the trunk. I lay in the darkness, sweating fear while I waited for Bradley to pull over and give me another jolt from the stun gun. Instead we gained speed. If we were approaching freeway velocity during rush hour it meant we were already out past Rancho Cucamonga. I would have to work fast. I fumbled open my toolbox and found the mini-flashlight.

In my business, I kept more lock picking gizmos than auto repair tools in my car trunk. Fishing through them for a handcuff key, I became aware that I had torn the scab off the bullet gouge along my arm. The pain brought back memories of the night I was shot, of wrapping Neiborsky's .22 Banker's Special in a rag and stashing it in the bottom of the toolbox. As soon as my hands were free, I fished out the compact Colt and unwrapped it.

The five unfired hollow points were of no immediate use. The metal seat springs between the trunk and the driver would deflect .22s. Even if I managed to put a lucky shot past them, all I'd get for my trouble would be a high speed crash. Waiting until Bradley stopped and opened the trunk was also not an option. My first exposure to sunlight would blind me. I tucked the revolver into my coat pocket and found a sturdy screwdriver.

It took some squirming to position myself where I could reach the trunk latch. I had to hold the light in my mouth to free both hands. The temperature had risen as we had come inland and my fingers were slippery with sweat. Judging from the diminished hum of the tires, we were well along the two-lane road to Sturtevant's by the time I was able to spring the mechanism. I lifted the trunk lid an inch. Sun through the narrow opening hit my eyes like an arc light. Before they could adjust, we bumped off the asphalt. Dust billowed behind us. We climbed the small rise and drifted to a stop. Ready or not, my chance had come. I threw up the trunk lid and scrambled out.

The idea was to make a run for it before Bradley could react. Not only was it not much of a plan, but I had grossly overestimated my ability to pull it off. My legs had lost circulation. Adrenaline was all that kept me on my feet. I was as close to sunblind as I could get. I had to squint my eyes almost shut to make out the hill behind Sturtevant's trailer. I took it on faith that the protective boulders and concealing scrub were still where I had seen them yesterday. And that I had enough head start to reach them. I ran like a drunken antelope.

"Sonafabitch!" Bradley yelled, and followed up with a string of prison yard profanity. Judging from the stress in his voice, he took it very personally when people didn't go along with his brilliant schemes.

The noise of his shotgun was almost insignificant out in the open country. Puffs of dry dirt rose in a cluster on the slope ahead and to my right. The Department of Corrections had spent its recreational budget on weight rooms to bulk up the thugs and had nothing left over for a skeet range where the killers could practice. Bradley would probably have Paige Lomax file suit as soon as he got back to L.A.

I could only hope the shot had scared some sense into Sturtevant. If he came down with delusions of courage and waddled out waving a gun, we'd both wind up dead. If he forted up and called 911, all I had to do was stay alive until the police came. I reached the base of the hill and scrambled for high ground and cover.

The terrain was steeper than it looked, the soil loose underfoot. I couldn't go straight up without slipping back. I had to angle across the slope. Sharp stones cut my right foot. I remembered the shoe I had left in the trunk, but I didn't know what I was going to do about it. Scrub branches whipped my arms and snatched at my legs. In spots they grew high enough to slap my face. I reached a boulder and collapsed behind it.

The late afternoon sun hung low enough over the horizon for the surrounding vegetation to cut the glare. Relative dimness let me open my eyes. I could hear Bradley, but the brush that had restored my vision kept me from spotting him. One thing was becoming clear. Overmatched and outgunned, I had to slow him down or I was dead.

"Bradley!" I yelled.

He didn't answer. The noise he had been making stopped. I could imagine him listening, trying to get a fix on me. I fumbled the short barreled Colt out of my pocket.

"Give it up, you moron! Sturtevant has called the cops by now."

That was just to make sure Sturtevant got the message. I didn't expect to scare Bradley. Based on what I'd heard and seen his head was full of demons telling him he had to be in control. Telling him he had to punish anyone who didn't obey. Movement appeared in the scrub below me. I caught a glimpse of him, head down, following my tracks. I used the boulder for an armrest and drew back the hammer of the little revolver.

I would have one shot, the instant he broke cover. Once he spotted me, the superior range of his shoulder gun would give him an unbeatable advantage. At thirty plus yards, I couldn't realistically expect to hit him. I just wanted to let him know I had a gun, hoping that would make him cautious.

He materialized out of the vegetation, fuzzy and wavering in my squint. The gun sights were in clear focus. I wasn't even aware of squeezing the trigger. The pop of the .22 surprised me. I was up and scurrying among the boulders immediately, dodging and climbing.

Backward glances showed no sign of pursuit. An idea seized me, half inspiration and half hallucination. Bradley was smart. He wouldn't chase an armed man. He would use his superior strength and endurance to get ahead of me and set up an ambush. He knew the ground. He had been here before, spying on Sturtevant. When I found my way out of the scrub and the rocks he would be waiting for me. I turned and stumbled headlong back down the hill.

I was exposed as soon as I broke cover, but if I could reach the trailer before Bradley could get a bead on me, I could fort up with Sturtevant. We could hold him off until the police arrived. It seemed like a workable plan until my feet went out from under me. I started out sliding, but the slope grew steeper and I began to roll. I flailed desperately, got my feet under me and then lost my balance and started the process all over again.

Bradley had seen it coming.

He was sitting at the bottom of the hill with his back against a lone pine, just waiting for me. He couldn't have positioned himself more perfectly. Gravity was taking me straight toward him. He just sat there with the combination gun across his lap and waited. I got a little control over my fall and slid the last few feet on my backside.

I sat staring at Bradley. He didn't move. The dust I had kicked up settled over both of us. Gradually it dawned on me that something was wrong with him. I began to wonder if he could see me. His eyes didn't look more than a millimeter deep. I pointed the .22 Colt at him.

He didn't do anything. I came up very carefully to a crouch and edged toward him. He didn't resist when I reached out and gingerly lifted the weapon off his lap. If it hadn't been for the tree at his back, he would have fallen over. The single round I had fired had taken him in the chest. I could see the tiny hole in his shirt. There was only a trace of capillary blood. His lungs were still in the process of collapsing, sucking everything inside.

Gravity had brought him here as it had brought me. He had known he needed help and his feet had followed the path of least resistance until he ran out of steam and had to sit down against the tree.

He had no breath to speak, but he managed to form the word, "Doctor," on his lips.

I got to my feet and limped off to find Sturtevant's trailer. We had come farther than I realized. I had to make my way up out of a swale and hike a couple of hundred yards. As I hobbled along, the last of my terror drained away and left me with an angry case of jitters. I stumbled up onto the porch beside the trailer.

"Sturtevant, it's Henry Spain. Open up. It's all over."

No response.

I banged on the door with the butt of the combination gun and yelled for a frustrated minute before I noticed what I should have seen at once. The cream colored Jeep was gone. Sturtevant wasn't home. I had shown up with the decisive bit of evidence to get his book re-issued. He would be in L.A., trying to get his hands on Neiborsky's statement. I limped down to the Volvo to find a lock pick that would get me into the trailer. Not that calling 911 would do Bradley any good. I had seen the creeping blue of cyanosis in his lips. He wouldn't last until the paramedics arrived. But if you were one of the good guys, you were supposed to call anyway. Then I remembered Eladio Aguilar, dying alone in a dark parking lot in East L.A. because he had wandered into the path of one of Bradley's schemes. I decided things were fine just the way they were.

Sturtevant could look after the undertaking duties. It was time he contributed something besides warped conspiracy theories. I locked the combination gun in the trunk and got behind the wheel. Dizzy from dehydration, I did well to get the car onto the two lane black top and keep it there. The accelerator pedal had grown needles. Holding pressure with my right foot was agony. Sore spots dictated how I sat. I was beginning to stiffen. Sweat pasted my clothes to my body. Shivering didn't help matters. The long drive back to L.A. gave me too much time to think.

I had just shot one of the men involved in the Aguilar killing. The police weren't likely to believe my tale of self defense. They were liable to think I had killed Bradley to cover my own complicity. I couldn't blame them. Not only was my story of being sent into East L.A. to look for a sixteen year old runaway on the night Aguilar was killed not very convincing, it also wasn't true. I had a pretty good idea now what really had happened to me. I also knew I had it coming.

I had gone into East L.A. without asking any of the obvious questions. I was kidding myself if I thought I was playing Galahad for Stevie. My one-nighter with Cassandra left no doubt what kind of creep I was. When opportunity knocked, I answered. I was no better than Paige or Sigrid or any of the other players. At least not until now.

I finally understood the situation I'd stepped into. I wasn't sure how much damage control I could put in place, but I knew I would never feel right if I didn't give it my best shot. In spite of the little voice reminding me that no good deed ever went unpunished.

CHAPTER 30

I woke next morning drenched in sweat. To get to sleep, I'd taken a pain killer left over from my last root canal. The prescription should have mentioned Technicolor nightmares. I was chasing sixteen year old Robbie Freegate when I realized I was being chased by a fleet of foreign luxury cars flying Jolly Rogers. Somehow I wound up in the middle of a sword fight. The pirates had been attacked by a gang in pin stripe suits. I was the only one without a cutlass, and nobody seemed to care how many pieces they were about to slice me into. I rolled out of bed grateful that my drug of choice was Jamaican rum.

Just touching the carpet with my right foot was excruciating. Balancing on one foot while I took a shower wasn't practical, so I filled the tub. Soaking felt good. Watching the water turn a progressively darker shade of pink didn't. I re-taped a nasty gouge just below my ribs. Based on the hole in the lower back of my coat, Bradley's shotgun charge hadn't missed quite as completely as I had thought.

The morning paper took the edge off my appetite for breakfast. A suspect had been apprehended in the murder of Eladio Aguilar. According to LAPD public relations, the arrest had resulted from good, old-fashioned police work. An alert officer had cited a car parked in a handicapped zone the night of the murder. Investigators had taken that information and painstakingly built their case. Patrol units were notified. One of them spotted the suspect in Century City and made the arrest. The story you have just read was true. Names have been withheld to protect the innocent. Dum-dah-dum-dum.

The suspect was almost certainly Davey Rimmer leaving the law offices of Berkut and Schroeder. After the episode in the garage, he was probably on the downside of a marijuana jag and not thinking too clearly. He might have blabbed about Bradley driving me out into the badlands to kill me.

The phone startled me out of my brooding.

"Officer Enright, Mr. Spain. I want to see you as soon as you can get here."

Panic was my first impulse, but if the law had found Bradley's body and connected me with his death, they wouldn't be phoning. They'd have the house surrounded.

"Ten o-clock fits my schedule," I said, not sounding as calm as I wanted to. "Does that work for you?"

"This is police business."

"Pardon me if I'm a few minutes late," I said, and hung up.

Thumbing my nose was a risk, but if I suddenly turned cooperative Enright might wonder why. I finished eating, loaded the dishwasher, limped out to the garage and ran nitro powder solvent through the shotgun tube of Bradley's combination gun and the barrel and two chambers of Neiborsky's .22 Colt.

The two weapons and the handcuffs in my trunk were the only physical evidence in my possession of what had happened between me and Victor Bradley. According to the US Constitution, I didn't have to volunteer evidence against myself. Under State law I could be prosecuted if I destroyed the evidence. Which put me in the Kafkaesque position of being required to safeguard stuff that could send me to prison. While the solvent soaked in, I called the law offices Berkut and Schroeder.

Roger Berkut didn't appreciate the interruption and he didn't like my tone of voice, but at least he took what I told him seriously enough to agree to an appointment as soon as the police finished with me.

Enright was in a foul mood considering he had Eladio Aguilar's killer in custody. I told him the source of my obvious injuries was none of his business, and the interview went downhill from there. Apparently Davey told the police he killed Aguilar out of fear that Bradley would kill him if he didn't, and stuck to his story. Enright had long since made up his mind that I knew more than I was telling. He demanded to know what had motivated Bradley. I told him I didn't want to speculate, which saved me from lying. His questions got more detailed. I wasn't surprised that the police had developed information I hadn't, but I was surprised by some of the things he asked me. I couldn't afford to blurt anything out, so I ended the festivities by insisting on knowing whether or not I was under arrest. Enright didn't have enough to hold me, and that ruined everything for him.

Berkut and Schroeder's receptionist winced at the side of my face that had been scraped raw sliding down the hill behind Sturtevant's trailer and gave me a sympathetic smile. She probably thought I was an accident victim looking for someone to sue.

A trim paralegal came out and asked me to follow her. I kept up as best I could. My right shoe was padded with all the gauze I could stuff in, but I still wasn't completely mobile. She let me into Roger Berkut's well-appointed corner office.

"Good Lord!" Berkut said in a voice that reeked of upper crust cultivation. Tall and imperially slim, he had a silvery pompadour that would be right at home in any boardroom. "What happened to you?"

"Exactly what I told you on the phone."

Berkut glanced at Jerry Freegate, who stood gazing bleakly out an expanse of tinted window, and coughed lightly to get his attention.

"Perhaps we could begin."

Two heavy chromium and leather chairs faced Berkut's chromium edged desk. I limped to one and settled in, grateful to be off my foot. Freegate smirked at my discomfort and took the other. Berkut sat facing us, savoring the authority of the desk. I had called the meeting, so I decided I was entitled to the opening remark.

"Mr. Berkut, I'm sorry you didn't get your money's worth on the surveillance."

He arched his eyebrows, but said nothing.

"These are lean and hungry times in the legal profession," I went on. "A juicy software piracy case like the one being mounted against El Camino would do wonders for your firm's revenue stream."

"I don't think I like the direction you're taking." His tone warned me that I would elaborate only at my own peril.

"You knew about the case because Peter Lomax works for one of the prospective plaintiffs. But it wouldn't be ethical for Paige Lomax to approach her husband to ask for the business. That would be tampering with another firm's attorney-client relationship. Feel free to jump in if I'm missing any legal niceties. Those are important because Paige Lomax's office e-mail is legally the property of Berkut and Schroeder. So you brought in a technician to read her e-mail without her knowledge to see if there was anything that would let you get a foot in the door."

"We have both a right and a responsibility to protect privileged communication," Berkut maintained.

I shook my head. "Your technician discovered someone was already reading it without anyone's knowledge. You hoped it was someone connected with the El Camino investigation checking out her husband. You had your technician use the intercept address to read that person's e-mail. When a message about a meeting in East L.A. turned up, you wanted the location staked out. You hoped to establish that a rival law firm was violating ethics by reading your privileged communication; to use that information to blackmail your way onto the El Camino legal team."

Tension in the tiny muscles of Berkut's poker face suggested that an indignant outburst was at war with the years of legal experience that were telling him to keep shut and let me spill everything I knew.

"As luck would have it," I continued, "Mr. Freegate's son chose that time to run away. If Mr. Freegate hired someone to stake out the East L.A. location to find his boy, it would look like you came by any information as the result of an innocent fluke. You would have preferred a national agency with lots of high tech surveillance goodies, but I guess Mr. Freegate was tired of standing in the great man's shadow. He insisted on hiring me."

Freegate sulked.

Berkut rippled his manicured fingers on the desk. "Is this in the form of a complaint, Mr. Spain?"

"No. I can't prove any of it. You dropped the whole thing when I found a murder instead of a meeting. But you did put me to a lot of trouble, and I wanted to establish a basis for the invoice I'll be sending you."

Berkut didn't like that. He was accustomed to deciding who got paid and when, and probably to stiffing anyone who didn't kiss his backside. On the other hand, his cancelled check would let him claim that I was working under privilege if any of his scheming surfaced later.

"Which brings us to Mr. Freegate's activities," I said.

Fury choked Freegate's voice. "Let me tell you something, Spain. My name, if I hadn't changed it, would be Gianni Frigati. I've got some hot Italian blood in my veins."

"So did Leonardo Da Vinci and Gallileo. Why don't you see if you can be as smart as they were?"

Freegate grabbed the arms of his chair like he was going to use them to launch himself at me.

Roger Berkut cleared his throat. "Gentlemen," he said in a strict orator's voice, "can we please discuss this civilly?"

Freegate gave his attorney and financial backer a nervous glance, then subsided.

"Mr. Spain?" Berkut asked.

"I presume you and Mr. Freegate have already talked?"

"Yes. We have."

"Then you know that he contracted with a parole client of Paige Lomax's to have me murdered."

"Not true," Berkut insisted.

"The parole client's name is Victor Bradley. As I told you on the phone, Bradley has already tried to carry through with the contract."

Berkut gave me a stern lecture. "In fact no such contract exists. Nor has Mr. Freegate ever attempted to instigate anything of the sort. It was Mr. Bradley who contacted Mr. Freegate and informed him, correctly or otherwise, that you and Mrs. Freegate were involved. He proposed that Mr. Freegate pay him to remove you. Now it is possible, in the emotion of the moment, that Mr. Freegate's natural shock at the allegation may have been mis-interpreted by Mr. Bradley as assent to the scheme. But no money or other consideration was ever paid."

"Save the legal technicalities for the Prosecutor. You may need them. The police have Bradley's accomplice in custody, and plenty of leverage to make him talk, if they ever get wind of this."

"Where is Mr. Bradley now?" Berkut watched and listened with senses I knew would pick up the stress of any lie.

"I haven't seen him since the attempt on my life."

"Do you know where he might have gone?"

"If you want me to find him for you, I'll prepare one of my standard contracts. Otherwise, he's police business."

"How much have you told the police?"

"Nothing."

"And if Mr. Bradley is apprehended, what do you propose to tell them?"

"As little as possible," I said. "Freegate's television exposure will escalate any domestic troubles into a media soap opera. I don't need that kind of advertising."

I thought I saw relief behind the triumph in Berkut's expression. That probably translated to his not wanting to risk having Freegate's hip customers learn the money they thought they were paying to one of their own was really going to a pompous old gas bag.

"Naturally," I said, "my silence assumes there won't be any more attempts on my life."

Freegate snarled, "You just keep away from Cassandra!"

"Your wife," I said, "came to me to discuss ways of discouraging your son from running away again. On the one and only night Davey Rimmer saw her at my home, there was no romantic contact between us."

I guessed that was pretty much the story Cassandra had given him. It wasn't the whole truth, of course, but there were times when candor was an over-rated virtue.

"Cassandra is all that really matters to me," he warned. "I'll do what it takes to keep her."

"Trusting her might be a good first step," I suggested. "And keeping your backside out of prison wouldn't hurt either."

Freegate sank deeper in his chair. Without the television panache he was just another ruggedly handsome doofus hoping the morning jog and the fashion consultant would keep him off the also-ran list a while longer. He was beyond talking to. I steeled myself against the pain in my foot and stood facing Berkut.

"You explain it to him. I'm late for an appointment with Paige Lomax."

I had finally found my way to the truth, and I was determined to confront her with it.

Chapter 31

A garrote of silence choked Paige Lomax's office. Peter and I each sat in one of the client chairs facing her desk. We might have been furniture ourselves for all the fuss we made. Paige devoured my report with a predator's eyes; no muscle of her face moved even a millimeter.

"There is a verbal addendum," I said when she was done. "I didn't learn about it until the police had me in for a talk this morning."

"A talk about what?"

"They were upset because I reported your mother-in-law's name as Cynthia Halston."

Peter blinked at me through the lenses of his rimless spectacles. "That is correct."

"Police investigation established that your mother's true name was Luise Marut. Her father edited a small anti-fascist newspaper in Germany. Her mother had left Norway one jump ahead of the police. When the Nazis came to power, daddy split for Mexico, leaving mama and Luise to follow as best they could. They got as far as Providence, Rhode Island, where mama fell in with a scam artist and went to prison as the result of a badger game. After that Luise was in and out of foster homes and correctionals. She broke probation on an armed robbery charge to come to Hollywood. With a fugitive warrant out for her arrest, she couldn't use her own name."

Enright had learned that and probably more when a cross-check on the name Cynthia Halston turned up a nineteen fifty six INS investigation. While he questioned me about it, a broader truth had dawned. After Ramona's dreams of stardom faded, she hadn't just sold her story to *Confidential.* She also went to Arthur

Mazmanian with everything she had learned in her years of living with Sigrid. Ramona's parentage had probably left her highly sensitive to the value of US citizenship. She knew Sigrid had never been naturalized, and that Sigrid's identity was based on a birth certificate pilfered when the real Cynthia Halston was committed to an institution for the criminally insane. Mazmanian took the information to the INS and demanded that Sigrid be deported.

To remain in the country, Sigrid needed a husband. One with US citizenship and preferably a little juice. Franklin Winter found her the perfect match in Harold Lomax. The INS wasn't about to irritate an FBI Agent over a minor immigration case. They closed Sigrid's file with a recommendation that no action be taken.

Angry color was rising in Peter's face when I finished, but Paige did the talking. "We've already established that Peter's mother came to Hollywood a naïve, star-struck teenager and gravitated to the wrong crowd."

"Star struck, yes," I conceded. "Naïve, no. She grew up around professional criminals."

"A nineteen year old high school drop-out could not have orchestrated a sophisticated extortion scheme."

"This was a trailer court badger game. The kind of behavior Luise Marut learned from her mother."

"Studio counsel would have made short work of anything that trivial," Paige insisted.

"How much do you know about military justice?"

The question surprised her. "Nothing. Few civilian attorneys do."

"Or did then. Lawyers who could fix a civilian rape charge between cocktails wouldn't know where to begin with a general court martial. And the studio, not the mark, would foot the bill for a settlement. Trevor got a salary he was probably worth anyway. Sigrid and Ramona were cast in cheap film roles that had to be filled by someone."

And for Gabriel Skidmore his coveted job in studio security. Skidmore had finally leveled with me when I called him from my office while I was putting the finishing touches on my report.

"Small time, small crime," I summed up.

Paige tapped one of her talons on the report. "You make some very serious accusations against Victor Bradley."

"Bradley saw you as more than a ticket to freedom. He wanted you on the City Council, as political protection for crimes he was planning."

"Evidence," she demanded.

"Bradley sent an accomplice to kill Alex Sturtevant. The accomplice murdered a medical student by mistake. The police have the accomplice in custody."

Peter could contain himself no longer. "Sturtevant's ridiculous accusations have been public for years."

"Why are they ridiculous?"

"My father wouldn't have lasted thirty two years in the FBI if his character weren't sound."

"Stand back from that for a minute. Look at the overall picture."

"What am I supposed to see?"

"Imagine you are in Saigon in April of 1975. The last defenses are crumbling. When Hue fell during the Tet offensive, more than five thousand government officials and supporters were massacred. Which would you rather get out of the country, your fortune or your backside?"

"If Sturtevant was wrong, why try to kill him?" he asked, rather than focus on his oversights.

"Sturtevant was right, short only one crucial fact. The Vietnamese didn't approach Winter. He approached them. As a general officer, he could make them believe had some say in who got on the helicopters. He sold them a ticket out in return for loading his Starliner with their gold."

"General Winter is a man of the highest integrity," Lomax protested.

"He was a soldier. Your mother presented him with an opportunity to deny resources to the enemies of his country and he took it."

"My mother?"

"She told him which Vietnamese to contact."

"That's ludicrous."

"She probably had a good idea of the situation in Saigon from communication she had with your father. Her old friend Ramona had a weakness for bad boys when she was younger. Members of organized crime who could provide names of Vietnamese nationals whose gold they laundered."

"You are speculating."

I knew it to a moral certainty. A year of combat in Vietnam taught me how much value money has when you're not sure if you'll ever see the sun rise again.

"The scheme was organized outside the country, because only people beyond the range of gunfire think in financial terms. And only Cynthia Lomax had the contacts."

"That proves nothing."

"Proof was never the issue. From day one this has been an exercise in public relations. *Vote Paige Lomax for Honest Government* wouldn't go down too well if the citizens learned your mother had made the family fortune extorting gold from corrupt politicians. That's a long way from Alex Sturtevant's allegation that your father was a minor player in some shadowy conspiracy that was no better than half believable even when it was fresh."

Peter Lomax stood and loomed over me. I thought for a minute he was going to kick my shin. He looked that peeved. But he settled on verbal assault.

"Spain, you are leaving this office. But before you go, I want an apology. You slandered my parents. You insulted my wife. You're not going to get away with it."

"Sit down, Mr. Lomax. I'm not through."

"Don't you—"

"Sit down, Peter," Paige said calmly. "Mr. Spain is going nowhere until he tells me what he said that got Roger Berkut in such an uproar."

Peter sat down.

"Well, Mr. Spain?"

"Berkut discovered that Bradley was reading your e-mail."

"Victor has no access to a computer. Or to the firm's network."

"Don't play naïve, Mrs. Lomax. Bradley stole a laptop, hacked in and learned about your plan to run for the Council. He learned you were worried about Alex Sturtevant, and about Harold Lomax saying the wrong thing to Stephanie St. John. So he hacked into Sturtevant's e-mail and learned Sturtevant was meeting her in East L.A. That's why he tried to have Sturtevant killed. He also learned about El Camino from exchanges between you and your husband and used his prison contacts to set up a hijacking."

"Did you make that allegation to Roger Berkut?"

"I didn't have to. Berkut had a technician review the network."

She conceded with the smallest possible smile. "It seems I owe Roger an apology. Of course, I'll terminate Victor as a client."

I didn't tell her she was a little late. "You should also know that Bradley accepted a contract from another Berkut and Schroeder client, Jerry Freegate, to murder me."

Her jaw tightened. That told me she knew Freegate was more than just a client, and Berkut stood to lose serious money if he got himself into trouble. It was the first real impression I'd made on her. I decided to press whatever advantage that gave me.

"It was a good con, Mrs. Lomax. It had me fooled for quite a while. But it's over now."

"Don't talk in riddles, Mr. Spain."

"Bradley knew too much about your problems. Far more than he could have gleaned from random snatches of e-mail. You had to feed him fairly long threads to lead him in the direction you wanted him to go."

Paige forced herself to silence, as Berkut had done before her, waiting for me to turn my cards face up.

"Bradley saw himself as the master manipulator. It never occurred to him that someone could be pulling his strings. You knew his record, and you counted on his picking up where he left off when he was shut away, with the added savvy of a computer science degree. All you needed was a sympathetic judge to sign an order moving him temporarily to Camelot while his parole hearing was being prepared."

She'd fed him enough to point him where she wanted, right down to summoning me to her office so he could get a look at me. If he scored, neither Sturtevant nor I would be able to expose her mother-in-law's past and the El Camino threat would be minimized. In any event, he'd be back behind bars in a month or so, totally dependent on her for his shot at parole and no evidence tying her to anything he'd done. I knew it but I couldn't prove it.

Peter cleared his throat. "I believe it was you who informed Paige of my mother's past."

"She already knew it. She said your mother was a nineteen year old high school dropout in 1944. She didn't get the high school dropout part from me, because I wasn't aware of it. And nineteen was the correct age for Luise Marut. The date on the Cynthia Halston birth certificate would have made her twenty one."

Paige put my report away in a drawer. "If one word of your allegations ever becomes public, you will be facing legal action for defamation, libel and slander. I will litigate you into the ground. Now get out of my office."

I did as I was told. As much as I wanted to see her in prison, it wasn't going to happen. The same fate that led me to kill the only witness against her had already decided her punishment. Her dreams of position and influence had turned to vapor. In a few days Roger Berkut would show her the door. She would give the obligatory interview to a sympathetic member of the press, explaining that she had made the agonizing but very necessary decision to be with her children during their difficult teen years, but that she would be back. That last part would be true. The Paige Lomaxes of the world were never really gone. They were just lurking.

I didn't waste any sympathy on Peter. A lot of his illusions had been shattered, but sooner or later everyone had to come to terms with the fact their parents had feet of clay. And when he did, I had no doubt he would go right back to being the same jerk he'd always been.

I had one more job to do before I went back to being the same creep I'd always been. It wasn't a job I was looking forward to.

CHAPTER 32

Stevie hadn't wanted to meet me where she taught flying. No privacy was the excuse; dark and shameful the subtext. The restaurant across from the airfield was Mexican, so I ordered the enchilada I hadn't gone for the night we met in East L.A.

Airplanes took off and landed every couple of minutes. Trainers doing touch and goes, fast personal cruisers, faded twin-engine models flying canceled bank checks and shinier ones off on rich men's fishing trips. An intricate ballet of escape and recapture. Man could soar briefly, but in the end gravity always won.

It hadn't caught up with Stevie yet. She was car-sitting six figures worth of powder blue Jaguar. Or so she informed me after she slid into the booth across the table, just in case I had any wrong ideas about the ride she'd pulled up in. She paid lip service to my damaged face, but she had other things on her mind.

"Iced tea, please," she said to dismiss the waitress and then asked, "What did you find out?" with a smile that hinted at provisional reinstatement on her sucker list if I could deliver.

She had drop dead gorgeous down to a science. A little make-up, a hint of Shalimar and a stray shirt button didn't sound like much, but when I confronted the real deal at a range of two feet, hormones replaced brain cells as the main source of ideas.

"Tell me about the night Harold Lomax died," I ordered before my nerve and common sense evaporated.

Her fleeting frown warned that my standing was shaky. "He said to take his car and catch a movie."

"Did you pick that night because you knew he wouldn't be carrying a gun?"

Wide eyes and a husky, "What?" tried to convince me she wasn't following my drift.

"Not even an insecure ex-fed like Lomax would have taken his gun to a formal dinner. The banquet hall might have a metal detector. He'd be embarrassed if he set it off in front of his stuffed-shirt friends."

Her voice became very quiet and precise. "Do you know what would happen if I let out a good scream?"

"Sure. Someone would call the police and we could discuss Lomax's death with them."

Skin at the base of her nostrils whitened.

"Stevie, you're a professional pilot. You knew your father's death was an accident. You weren't after Lomax for murder. You were trying to shake him down for a share of the loot. That's what this has been about from day one. Lomax and Winter got rich. Your mother was left to raise a family on whatever the lawyers hadn't scavenged from her settlement. You grew up stewing over the Sturtevant book while other girls had money to go to the prom and wear the latest fashions. Your first chance to cash in died with Lomax. Winter was a tougher nut to crack. You tried making waves at the NTSB. When that went nowhere, you contacted Sturtevant to learn what he knew about the old General that he hadn't put in the book. You arranged to meet in East L.A., which is where I came in. Henry Spain, professional sucker. You aimed me at Winter to see what I could find."

Her eyes were blue ice. "I went to the prom," she informed me. "I had a killer gown."

"Where did you go the night Lomax died? Some cocktail lounge to work up your courage?"

"I wasn't drunk."

"You drove back with your mind made up to confront him. When he got into the car, you made your pitch."

"I just told him who my dad was."

"What did he do?"

"He got this scared look on his face, bailed out and took off. So I guess you're not as smart as you think you are."

"Did you chase him?"

"All I did was turn on the headlights to see which way he went."

To Lomax the lights had probably been the harbinger of impending pursuit. Confused by age and liquor, he had run for his life and lost it in the process. The enchilada started to curdle in my stomach.

"Did you see it happen?"

She gave her head a tense, tiny shake. "I heard it. I mean the tires and the horn and the car hitting him."

"What did you do?"

"I ran to look, but there were a lot of people. Some police and security from the banquet told us to move back." A helpless shrug described the situation better than any words could have. "I went home. I didn't know he'd died until I saw it on the late news."

"You also didn't contact his estate about returning his Bentley."

"I wasn't going to keep it."

"You were if you could get away with it."

Indignation lit her eyes. Men didn't talk to her that way. Before she could rip into me, her iced tea arrived. She composed herself with a look that suggested she had a perfect right to Lomax's Bentley and anything else she could get her hands on.

"I can do arithmetic," she said when the waitress was gone. "I know how much gold they had to sell to get as rich as they are. They couldn't do that without attracting attention. They would have gone to prison if their friends in the power structure hadn't turned a blind eye."

"Winter's prison is freedom and victory."

She looked at me like I was crazy. Maybe I was.

"Most of us die somewhere short of our life's goals," I said. "We still have something to struggle for right up to the end. Winter spent his life fighting communism. When the Berlin Wall came down, so did his reason for being. He had nothing left but years of aimless shuffling."

"You're just making stupid excuses for him. You never found out anything."

"Actually, I did."

I told her the real story behind the Sturtevant book. She wasn't impressed.

"Do you expect me to believe it was all the doing of some woman I never heard of?"

"It's simple enough. Sigrid had never had anything or been anyone, so she grabbed what she could and basked in the reflected glow of other people's respectability."

"There was nothing respectable about Harold Lomax and General Winter. They were two slimy crooks who were in the right place at the right time."

It had bothered me at first that Lomax and Winter just happened to be in Saigon together, but I had since realized it probably wasn't a coincidence. Both were senior men in their organizations, with some say in their postings. When they went overseas, they would want to be among their cronies so they could protect each other's reputations and careers.

"Which brings us to why the man we found in East L.A. was killed."

I told Stevie of Paige Lomax's fear that she might learn the truth from a senile Harold Lomax and shatter the illusion of respectability Paige needed to support her political ambitions. I told her how Paige tried to use Victor Bradley's twisted ambitions to remove the threat.

"Bradley's scheme was never more than a pathetic prison yard fantasy, but that didn't stop him from sending Davey Rimmer to East L.A. with instructions to kill Alex Sturtevant. Or Rimmer from mistakenly killing Eladio Aguilar."

"That's not my fault." She took a sip of her tea. It didn't seem to help. There wasn't enough tea in the world to drown survivor guilt. "They took advantage of my dad. I just wanted to pay them back."

We both knew it was about the money, but that wasn't an argument I could win, so I kept my mouth shut.

She stared bleakly into her glass. "Well, at least now there'll be some justice. No more of that hoo-hah about statute of limitations. They have to put General Winter on trial."

"I'm afraid not," I said, and explained it to her as best I could based on what I knew and what I had gleaned from my talk with Enright. With no tail number or freight manifest, there was no way to prove the Starliner that landed in California had taken off from Saigon, and no way to link Franklin Winter to the murder of Andrew Fisher, which he probably had never known about anyway.

The crimes that could be proven would work their way through the system to a foregone conclusion. Benjamin Neiborsky's age and years of alcohol dependency made him a potential medical burden the State could ill afford. For his part in Sigrid Helstrom's homicides, he would receive a short prison term with a long parole tail. Davey Rimmer's best chance to minimize his own prison time was to blame everything on Victor Bradley and keep his mouth shut.

I didn't tell Stevie that Bradley wouldn't be found any time soon. I'd received an urgent voice mail from Sturtevant. He was going east to show Neiborsky's statement to his publisher. He needed everything I had to get *Blood Money* revised and reissued. And would I please e-mail it. His phone had been disconnected and his trailer was already on the way back to Phoenix.

Stevie gave me one of her disappointed looks. "Isn't there anything you can do?" she asked, and waited for me to rise to the occasion.

"Absolutely. I can testify for the prosecution when you're charged with involuntary manslaughter in Harold Lomax's death."

"I didn't kill him," she snapped, then remembered where she was and glanced around to see if anyone was listening.

"It's not about justice, Stevie. It's about scarfing up all the money you can and then hanging on for all you're worth. If you declare yourself into the game, you'll be a target for all the other players. You were present at Harold Lomax's death with motive for extortion. Winter and the Lomax family will pressure the Prosecutor into charging you. Even if you're not convicted, you'll be ruined professionally and financially."

"What do you care?"

"Usually I don't. Most times I'm what you saw the night we met. A dirty old man trying to connect with a hot chick. But every so often I have to pull my head up out of the sewer, just to prove I'm still part of the world around me."

"Men should never get philosophical," she decided. "It ruins them for anything else."

She left me as she had found me, a couple of weeks older and not a whole lot wiser. There was nothing more I could do. The killers were either dead or headed for prison. The schemers had come away empty handed. A few sharpshooters wound up richer than they should have, but cutting corners and bending rules was par for the course in L.A. I had no particular right to expect Stevie to be any different.

I didn't expect to see her again. The last runaway teenage girl I'd tracked down had called me a Dorkasaurus. I probably looked about the same to someone Stevie's age.

I didn't expect to see Cassandra Freegate again either, but I thought of her when Jerry came on TV that evening to wheedle the upwardly mobile into cashing in their stock options to buy his latest model. All it did was remind me how far I'd isolated myself. I shut it off and put *Ambush Road* in the VCR.

I had seen hundreds of black and white movies. Until now they were just entertainment. The images flickering by weren't real people with real lives. They were immortal characters, frozen forever in the same choreography. But after I'd seen close up the price of celluloid mummification, the fantasy paled in comparison to the stories of the people who brought films to life. *Ambush Road* ended with Sigrid standing at a funeral in the rain, weeping softly with a muted horn in the background.

Pure Hollywood, but somehow it seemed appropriate.

END

0-595-30133-9